P. CURRY

Calliope of Atalan

The American Dream

Contents

I

The World Outside My Window

Trapped In A Box

As a cold and eerie mist permeated the air, giving way to a thick fog over the Atlantic Ocean, one would have a hard time believing this was the first day of spring. Draped in a red poncho, I carefully leaned upon the boat's railing as it neared Maeonia Peninsula and Chenab Island. We pulled in closer, and the fog began to clear somewhat, giving way to a sprawling, modern ruin. I can't help but shed a tear as I look upon the dark and dilapidated buildings, eerily lifeless beaches and a collapsed bridge.

"Behold, the ruins of the city-state of Atalan," the tour guide began elaborating to the tourists who curiously looked on. They all crowded around me on the railing, pulling out their cameras and smartphones to take pictures while I remained still, continuing to look on silently. A lump slowly formed in my throat when suddenly, out of the corner of my eye, I caught wind of a familiar glow. I turned my head towards the island on the north side of the collapsed bridge, where, much to my surprise, the skyscrapers still remained in a hauntingly dark and eternal silence, only to see the glimmer of the red light.

"It's so creepy how that red light still works even though the city's been abandoned for over twenty years," the girl next to me said, snapping a photo with her iPhone. I can't help but to think the same thing, as I start to listen in on other's observations.

"To think, this place used to be a big, vibrant city like New York and Chicago! What the hell happened?!"

"Men having too much money, power and hatred in their hearts, that's what happened here. Such a tragedy."

"Some people say it's all that girl's fault."

"You'd really believe that with all the good she's done for the world in the years since!? Don't be ridiculous!"

"Don't you remember the book we read in high school? *Atalan: A Revolution Deferred*? She laid out the truth of what really happened! Come on, man!"

I began to chuckle to myself after hearing this exchange. Little did they know, the author of that book was standing right next to them. I am Calliope Thessaly, the leader of the Atalan Revolution or the girl who destroyed Atalan, depending on whom is asked. The fall of Atalan is deeply intertwined with my own story.

I looked towards the red light once more and close my eyes, only to open them to a television screen where two girls dressed like clowns danced in front of their ringmaster with a flipped press curl. It was a news report about yet another successful party at the House of Peloponnesian. As revelers gushed over how much they enjoyed the spectacle, the newsreel shifted to yet another shiny, office building under construction in the Atlantic Colony; Atalan's Downtown. The hopeful glimmer of the building transitioned into the flashing lights of a police car as the news went on to report another homicide in one of the public housing developments in South Atalan.

Again I closed my eyes, only to smile and laugh with people as I held shopping bags and avoided paparazzi, like a movie star in The Atlantic Colony. Bathing in the sun on the shores of Santorini Beach, my dark, ebony skin glowed and my long, thickly curled hair bounced as I bobbed my head to the music and danced raucously at one of the infamous bacchanals of The Cascade.

The newspapers flew off the shelves, imploring everyone to read all about it. The televisions in all the living rooms described it at length. In the summer of 1992, Atalan was a mad house in all the right ways. The metropolis literally shimmered at night. The top heavy buildings in the Atlantic Colony were more intimidating than ever. The parties were extraordinary. Artists were at their most creative. Immaculate statues and fountains dotted the landscape. Architecture, entertainment and trade, the three tiers which made up the holy trinity of our city-state's economy, were booming. And the only way they could go from there was up.

Still, reporters lamented how the class divide was stronger than ever. The rich got richer. The poor got poorer. The crime and poverty rates were at the worst they had ever been. Drug use, gang violence, organized crime and prostitution were rampant. And then, there was I, who had merely only observed it all from the windows of my house in the polis of Auburn.

My family, the House of Thessaly, had lived in a beautiful coral house with seven bedrooms that looked straight out of Santorini itself, with wide square windows, several small balconies with gated barriers, a patio covered in arches that wrapped around the entire facade, and a large, round white dome on the top. Being of Upper Noble standing, we were afforded a great wealth of privilege within Atalan with only the Royals and Deities being more privileged.

And yet, for unbeknownst reasons, my parents forbade me from venturing too far from our home. I had four siblings, two of whom were younger, and all had more freedom than I had. At the age of fifteen, I barely even knew Auburn, let alone the rest of Atalan. I had never even been to an actual school.

I opened my eyes and sighed as I turned off the television and made my way back to my room. For years, I would perch myself on my window sill each night, just to glimpse at the hometown I hardly knew. A view of the glistening skyline of the Atlantic Colony, forming a sort of cave over the revolving, red light that signaled the entrance to The Acropolis peeking through.

"Calliope, are you sittin' up at that window *AGAIN*!?" I heard a voice say behind me.

I turned around, only to see Brutus standing at the doorway to my room. On the stocky side, with chiseled arms and a potbelly, his appearance was that of a stereotypical pretty boy, with hazel eyes, a head adorned with loose curls and a light brown complexion.

"Yes, I am sittin' up at this window again," I snidely replied.

"I don't see why, it's like opening the refrigerator every hour. Ain't nothin' changed," he said. I couldn't help but roll my eyes. His boorish attitude never failed to get under my skin.

"Man, leave her alone, you know she never gets out anyways," my brother Julius said, walking behind him. Aside from body shape and build, my eldest brother Julius was the complete opposite of Brutus, with an ebony complexion, a hi-top fade, dark brown eyes and a far more pleasant demeanor.

I turned over to Julius, smirked, and exclaimed, "Thank you very much Julius!" Brutus just rolled his eyes and walked to his room, while Julius walked into my room and sat on my bed.

He looked at me with his sweet, brown eyes and asked, "How does the city look tonight?"

"It looks... lovely. As always," I answered with an unsure tone. In all honesty, I didn't know how to reply to that question.

For years, all I had done was gaze upon the light and the mountainous, concrete structures that stood guard. I wanted to know more.

Julius chuckled before saying, "Alright then. Just wanted to check up on you, good night!"

"Good night," I said to him, watching him walk out of my room. I looked out my window for a few minutes more before closing it and going to sleep for the night. The next day, I rolled out of bed and ran my fingers through my long, tightly-coiled, curly hair. After that, I woke up my younger siblings, Isis and Atum, and we walked down the curved, marble staircase under the dome of our house to the bright and airy living room of our house. My mother, Demeter, loved plants and put them everywhere. And she always woke up very early every morning, to make breakfast.

It was always a pleasure to see her in the kitchen. Her eyes gleamed like black diamonds and her skin was beautiful and mahogany. She loved to hum while making breakfast and open all the windows in the pink, retro-styled kitchen of our home no matter how windy how it was.

"Babies, come close these windows before my grits fly away," she said to the three of us with a laugh. We closed the windows and proceeded to set the breakfast table like normal. We sat down and waited for her to finish breakfast, as she shook her hips to whatever song was playing in her head.

Isis sat on my right hand side. She was a very quiet girl who always had a smile on her face, with skin like mahogany, long, coiled locks and Demeter's eyes. Atum on the other hand, who sat on my left hand side, was basically a slim, younger version of Brutus.

"I don't want anyone to take a single bite before your father and older brothers get here," she told us in a stern, but sweet tone. It was always hard to resist her breakfast once it was finished. One couldn't help but drool at the sight of the spread, featuring buttered grits with cheese, cayenne-pepper spiced eggs and smoked sausage links. There was also a bowl of fresh fruit from the garden and fluffy biscuits covered in gravy. A tall stack of thin flapjacks with butter pecan syrup on the side towered over the pitcher of fresh orange juice which she always squeezed herself.

A few minutes later, my father, Pan, walked into the kitchen. In a crisply ironed brown blazer and a pair of black slacks, topped off with a brown felt hat, he exuded an aura of old-fashioned cool. He was a tall, but slim man with dark hazel eyes, loose coils adorning his head and light, sepia-toned skin.

"Good morning family!" he said cheerfully before giving each of us a kiss on the forehead, as usual.

"Good morning, Pan!" Demeter greeted enthusiastically, only for him to reply with a quick, impersonal nod of the head. Her bright, vibrant makeup did nothing to hide her solemn eyes as she sighed and went back to wiping down the counter. As he took a seat, I felt someone rub all over my head. I lightly smacked the hand away, only to hear Julius' laughter.

"Julius! You messed up my hair!" I exclaimed.

"Just run your fingers through it like you always do and you'll be fine," he replied, as he took a seat between Isis and Dad. A minute later, a shirtless Brutus walked into the kitchen, letting out a long yawn before taking the flapjack on top of the stack and dipping it into syrup.

"Brutus! How many times do I have to remind you to put clothes on before coming down to breakfast? AND to not eat flapjacks with your hands?" Mom asked him.

"Mama, its Brutus," I said nonchalantly, which made everyone else laugh while Brutus continued to eat his flapjack without a care in the world. After saying grace, we all dug into breakfast and began to talk.

"So, the school year is coming to a close. I assume everyone did well this year, yes?" Mom inquired with a sweet, relaxed tone.

"Yup! I'm going to graduate with flying colors!" Julius assured enthusiastically.

"I'm sure I did fine. All my teachers love me," Isis answered with a giggle.

"I hate to break it to you, but I think I'm going to have to repeat the fourth grade for the next five years!" Atum joked, as everyone aside from Brutus and Dad burst out laughing.

"Eh, I did alright I guess," Brutus groaned.

"I always have too much time on my hands, so I'm sure I'll have straight A's as usual," I commented. I then winked and smiled, but everyone just looked to me with discomfort before they went back to eating. Pan, who appeared to be deep in thought all morning, stood up and tapped his glass to grab everyone's attention.

"Family, I have an announcement," he said solemnly, "We're going to have to move. By next week."

I couldn't help but smile. I was enthralled with the prospect of seeing another part of Atalan. Hopefully it would be the Atlantic Colony. The rest of the family didn't appear to be so thrilled. Atum just stared as his jaw dropped in shock. Isis and Julius also stared with blank expressions of indifference. Brutus went back to eating as if nothing happened, while Mama, with a slight scowl in her eyes, clearly wasn't amused.

"Another secret, Pan?" she asked with slight irritation.

"How could it be a secret when I didn't know we had to move until last night? Mr. Peloponnesian told me over the phone."

"For years, you've been having these secret talks with that man, over god knows what. I can understand not involving your children, but at least tell your wife!"

He took a bite of his pancakes before he snidely remarked. "Try working my job one of these days. Maybe then you'll see why I can't tell you everything.

"Where are we going to be moving?!" I butted in, hoping it would relieve some of the tension at the breakfast table.

Dad took another sip of his orange juice, put the glass back down on the table, and answered, "Griffin."

I felt my heart sink as the smile on my face vanished. Far removed from Auburn, Griffin was even further from the Atlantic Colony and the red light.

"GRIFFIN???" everyone at the table yelled in unison.

"Yes," Dad answered. "My business is needed there."

"Your business is needed there? What kind of business? You're not even considering the rest of your family! Your kids have to start new lives and make new friends all over again. And I still have two businesses to run right here in Auburn! What about them?" Mom shouted at him as her nose and eyes tensed up.

"Me and Mr. Peloponnesian are going to have another meeting in a few days. He will explain everything and we'll get it all sorted out."

Mama groaned. "There you go again with that 'Me and Mr. Peloponnesian' thing again. Are you even listening to yourself?"

"If you don't want to listen to me, then that's quite alright. I'm going to work!" Dad yelled, taking one last sip of orange juice before he put his felt hat back on and stormed out of the kitchen.

Mama Demeter stood up and exhaled. "I apologize for that. I never wanted our problems to be aired out in front of all of you like that."

"It's alright. We always heard y'all arguing at night anyway," Julius nonchalantly replied as the rest of us nodded in agreement.

Mama Demeter let out another sigh. "Well, I'm sorry for that too. I just *can't* with that man sometimes. Finish your breakfasts and get ready for school."

"It's funny Mama would say we all have to start over making new friends. Calliope don't know anybody!" Brutus said obnoxiously as we finished breakfast.

"Man, why you always gotta be so rude to her?" Julius asked.

"Hey, it's true!" Brutus answered whilst laughing. "She don't got any friends!"

"She got Herc," Julius retorted.

"So she know the maintenance boy over at the House of Peloponnesian, but that doesn't mean she knows any *actual* Peloponnesians."

Julius smacked his lips. "Like she would get along with any of them anyway."

"I don't know, dude. I think her and the boy in blue could be best friends."

As I was walking to the kitchen sink, I couldn't help but to pause when I heard Brutus say "the boy in blue." I began to wash my plate in the sink as I remembered our encounter. I closed my eyes and re-imagined the hazy, dusk sky. Bathing the Garden of Artemis in an amber glow, as I wrote away in my notebook, I turned to my left to see a boy, dressed head to toe in blue, approach me. He was all smiles as he sat down next to me under the gazebo. He looked at me eagerly as I did the same.

"You know, I still don't know your name," I chuckled.

"I already told you... I'm the boy in blue," he laughed.

"I guess," I replied, "Do you want to hear another poem?"

"I'd like that," he said.

I opened my eyes, ridding myself of the daydream, and turned to Brutus. "What boy in blue?"

"Adonis Peloponnesian, of course! Who else?" Brutus exclaimed in reply, while everyone else in the kitchen just stared at me curiously.

"Oh," I said. As memories of the mysterious friend I had a year prior flashed across my mind, it had never once occurred to me he could have been a Peloponnesian. I just shook my head and dismissed it as a mere coincidence before I sighed and went back to washing my plate.

The Garden of Artemis

As soon as home school was over, I always made sure to spend at least an hour in The Garden of Artemis. Writing book in hand, I would either sit at the gazebo with the golden trellis in the middle of the park or just lay down in the grass and write away. The park was always its prettiest in the summertime. There were butterflies of many different hues everywhere. Pink and violet tulips, dandelions and red and orange lilies dotted the landscape. Since it was the last day of school, I knew the park would soon be teeming with life. For years, it had been my only exposure to life in Atalan, and I cherished every moment seeing the many different faces and what they were up to.

"Hi Calliope," I heard a high-pitched, childlike voice say. I looked up from my notebook to see Julius holding hands with his girlfriend, Bolina, a short, slightly plump girl with a light ochre shade of skin. She had the most adorable smile, gentle, brown eyes and a voice like a hummingbird.

"Hey there Bolina!" I replied.

"What are you up to?" she asked me.

"Just basking in the garden, writing as usual," I answered.

Julius laughed and said, "Yeah, like she always does, little miss nosy!"

Bolina and I joined in on his laughter before the two of them went about their way. I went back to writing but before I knew it there was yet another distraction.

"School's out *forever*!" I heard a deep voice with a strong, southern-style drawl say. It was Perseus, a friend of Brutus's who was short and skinny with a dark sepia skin tone, a floppy and messy afro and a face similar to a pit bull.

I looked up from my notebook again and saw him walk into the park with Brutus. He flashed a peace sign in my direction and I waved back as he and Brutus walked towards the back of the park, likely in search of somewhere to smoke.

I returned my attention back to my pink notebook, adorned with drawings of yellow hibiscus flowers and a yellow strap to keep the book closed. I continued to get lost in a sea of words about dreams, desires and everyday people before closing it and putting the notebook to the side. I turned over on my back in the field and stared at the golden red sky of twilight above, seconds away from dozing off.

"OOGA OOGA BOOGA," a deep, exaggerated voice chanted above me. I opened my eyes and looked up to see Herc, being a prankster as always. A tall guy of slightly muscular and athletic build, with dark, bistre skin, a short afro and copper brown eyes, his smile always had the ability to light up my day. He always opted for simple color schemes in all of his clothing, wearing either black, white or some combination of the two, aiding in his mastery of stealth and disguise.

"You always sneak up and try to scare me, but it's alright, cuz it's my favorite time of day," I said to Herc as I stood up and gave him a hug.

"Good, cuz it's mine too," he replied, which caused both of us to laugh.

"So, how was work today?" I asked him after we finished our little fit of laughter.

"Eh, same ol', same ol'. As long as I do everything they need me to do around the house without any of them bothering me, then it's all good as far as I'm concerned."

"Bother you? I'm not sure I follow," I said with a raised eyebrow.

Herc scoffed and rolled his eyes before he said, "The Peloponnesians ain't all they cracked up to be, Calliope. Not very pleasant people to be around at all."

"So why do people always say you need to know them?" I asked in a somewhat rhetorical tone, since I didn't have any desire in getting to know them in the first place.

"It's just a status thing, girl! You see how they throw those wild and crazy parties twice a month, right? But if you actually went to one of those parties, they're never anywhere to be found. I know from experience. So I betcha ninety percent of the people claiming to know Peloponnesians don't know them at all – they just think they got the right to say they know one because they went to a party there."

"Mhm," I replied with a smirk as I nodded my head. Despite my lack of interest in getting to know any of them, I had to admit, none of that changed my interest in seeing one of the famed Peloponnesian parties for myself.

Herc continued his rant. "Hermes is the only one you ever see at the parties. Ol' pompous ass."

"Are none of them decent people?" I asked.

"Well, the youngest daughter, Athena, she's super image-obsessed. Goes shopping after school every day, and won't be caught dead without her makeup or labels on her clothes, but she's really nice. Oh and Adonis, he's a cool dude. Gotta say he's on the mysterious side though," Herc answered.

I sat in the gazebo with Herc and pondered about all of it, I got a sudden feeling of being watched. I looked up and turned my head towards the House of Peloponnesian. I took a closer look at one of the balconies that looked directly over the Garden of Artemis. There was no one standing on the moss-covered, column-enclosed balcony, and the iron-gilded doors leading to the room of whomever was closed, but the light blue drapes behind the door were slightly askew, as if someone were peering out.

"What are you looking at?" Herc asked. In a mild daze, I lifted my hand up and pointed at the balcony. Once Herc turned to look at it, the drapes were no longer askew.

Herc looked back at me, laughed a hearty laugh. "So, they can't look out their window or something?"

"They? Who are you talking about?" I asked in reply with raised eyebrows.

"I don't know who I'm talking about. But whoever it was, they should be allowed to look out their window as much as they'd like!"

"I... I felt like they were looking at us though" I replied.

"Well how do you think people feel when you look out your window all the time?" Herc asked me with another laugh.

"Ugh, whatever," I answered.

The two of us sat in the park until the golden red, twilight sky transitioned into a romantic blue, evening sky with the lights of the Atlantic Colony glistening over the horizon. The light show of the red light was beginning its rounds for the night. We said our goodbyes and made our ways to our homes.

As I walked to my house, a shiny, golden, Jeep Wrangler drove by. As the song *Jump* by Kris Kross played, a passenger from the vehicle yelled out, "Party at the House of Peloponnesian this weekend! Caribbean theme!"

I gave a half-smile as they drove past. It was nice to know, but I wouldn't have been able to go either way. Mom told me the Peloponnesian party was the most disgusting thing she had ever seen, and dad expressly forbade me from ever going there.

As I walked into the white, marble double-doors of the house, expecting to smell a freshly-cooked meal while my family talked at the kitchen table, I didn't smell or hear a thing. All was silent downstairs. The lights weren't even on. Put off by the sight, I walked upstairs to see what everyone was doing.

As I made my way up the staircase, a strange vertigo effect took over me. With each step I took, it felt as if the top of the staircase kept pulling back. My heart was sinking. The silence of the house was deafening. The darkness of the house was blinding.

When I reached the top of the staircase, I paused for a quick breath. The walk up the staircase had never made me winded before. I looked down the hallway, and just like downstairs, it was dark and completely silent. I made my way down the hallway, growing more disturbed by the second with how inactive everything was. As I neared the door to the bathroom, I heard the toilet flush and the sink go on and off. The door opened and out came Brutus, with drowsy, reddened eyes, laughing for no apparent reason.

He turned to me and started to laugh even more boisterously. "I cooked up somethin' real nice just now. Feelin' five pounds lighter."

I stared at him sideways, confused about what he was trying to say. My nose tensed up when I got a whiff of the odor coming from the bathroom.

"Ew! Brutus!" I exclaimed, covering my nose as he continued to laugh loudly while he walked across the hall and into his room.

Well, at least Brutus was being his usual self, I thought.

I walked down the hallway a little further towards Julius's room. Peering into the cracked door, I saw him and Bolina, both fast asleep as she embraced him like a teddy bear. I smiled at the sight of the two lovebirds. I turned a corner to get to the longer half of the hallway, where the other four bedrooms were. The door to Atum's room was open and the light on. I walked towards it and looked in, to see him and Isis talking.

I knocked on the door to let them know of my presence and asked, "Hey you two, how is everything going?"

"Not very good," Isis said with a somber tone.

Both of them appeared to be very anxious, with Atum biting his lips and Isis's eyes being restless with worry. I walked into Atum's room and sat on his red and black checkered racecar bed.

"What's been going on since I've been in the garden?" I asked sternly.

"I think Mama is still upset over what happened this morning. When me and Isis came home, she wasn't cooking, cleaning or even nursing her plants. She was just sitting on the couch, sipping a glass of wine. She said 'hi' to us when we walked in and then went back to staring off into space," Atum answered with an anxious tremble.

My eyes widened. "Was she playing her Motown oldies at least?"

"No, she wasn't even doing that. It's like she wasn't even there on the inside," Isis answered while Atum nodded his head.

"Where is she now?" I asked with a gulp.

"She just went into her room and closed the door about an hour ago. Dad's not home yet either," Isis answered.

"This is the spookiest night I've ever seen in this house," Atum added with an unsettled voice and disturbed eyes.

Having heard enough, I got off the bed, left their room and walked to the end of the hallway to the master bedroom. I decided to put my ear against the closed door first before walking in. To my horror, I heard my mother on the other side of the door, softly, but hauntingly, sobbing away.

With no hesitation, I opened the door and saw her sitting on her canopy bed with one tissue in hand and a small pile of tissues on the floor. I ran into the room, sat on the bed next to her and promptly embraced her for support.

She put her arm around me and said, amidst her tears, "I really appreciate you for trying, Calliope. But a simple hug won't make this heartache go away."

"I know, Mama. But I'll do whatever I can to help. Would you like to tell me about it?"

She sniffled. "Not right now. I need to be alone. But if you'd like to know, I will tell you all about it when I calm down."

"Okay then," I said. I wanted to stay there with her, but I respected her wish to be alone.

As I walked out of the room, I turned back to her and said, "Let me know if you need a shoulder to cry on, okay?"

"Will do, Calliope. Will do. Thank you for trying to bring warmth into a cold room," she said. She laid down on the bed, pulled the translucent, white curtains over it and continued her sobbing. I looked back at her and sighed. I had always wished I could have done more to help her, but I was just a naive and oblivious young girl at the time. I walked out of her room and closed the door behind me. I looked back down the hallway and saw that Atum had turned off his light and closed his door, presuming that he and Isis had both gone to sleep. I figured it was probably time for me to go to bed for the night as well.

I walked into my room, turned on the light, and sighed yet again. The curtains, sheets and just about everything else was awash in some shade of red. I closed the door behind me and put down my notebook down as I changed into my pajamas. I sat down on the crimson chaise in front of my window and perched my arms on the window sill. I couldn't help but smile as I looked out and gazed away at the dazzle of the Atlantic Colony, while the red light and its revolution beckoned from underneath its caverns.

I gazed upon The House of Peloponnesian next door, which was especially lively on the eve of another one of its extravagant and rambunctious parties, which had occurred twice per month, every month, for an untold amount of years. In striking contrast to my house, the House of Peloponnesian was brightly lit and quite noisy, as if a party were being had in preparation for another one.

The side which faced our house was mostly covered in dark green moss, with three balconies jutting out and looking over the Garden of Artemis. The house was topped with two tall and imposing Corinthian pillars; statues of snarled griffins adorning their peaks. They appeared to look down at the entrance to the house, like guardians that were always ready to take out any intruder. While I saw a bright, radiant glow emanating from the front of the house, large trees obscured the rest of the view. The only other thing I knew about it was that it was set back almost a quarter of a mile away from the street. The space between the house and the street was a gated driveway, with a replica of the Colossus of Rhodes, torch in hand and looking north towards the Atlantic Colony and the Acropolis, standing guard over those very gates.

I closed my eyes and imagined I was wearing a sparkling, red dress while sitting in the back of a limousine. The driver honked as we sat in line, waiting to enter the gates. Once we pulled up, all eyes were on me as I walked up the staircase and into the foyer. A feather and headdress wearing showgirl danced while standing guard at the entrance to the ballroom. The revelers were all hooting and hollering, feeling unbearable tension as they waited to enter. Like a sphynx whose riddle had just been answered, she smiled before she stepped to the side and the dazzling light blinded us all.

I opened my eyes once more, just to realize I was still in my bedroom. A space that was warmer, safer and more comfortable for me than the house next door, but likely nowhere near as much fun. I closed the window and sighed before I got in the bed and went to sleep.

An Uneasy Morning

When Isis, Atum and I made our way downstairs the next morning, it was the most inactive morning at the House of Thessaly we had ever seen. A whiff of flapjacks, sausage links or grits was nowhere to be found. None of mama's humming. The windows in the kitchen were closed and the olive drapes that hung over them were eerily still. It was almost as if our house had been abandoned, with the three of us left behind.

While Mama taught me to cook when I was younger, I was nowhere near as good as she was, but I knew that after yesterday she was in no mood to cook. I told Isis and Atum to sit on the couch, turned the TV to *Rugrats* for them to watch and made my way into the kitchen to start making breakfast. About twenty minutes into preparing breakfast, I heard Brutus walk into the kitchen, letting out a long, slow yawn with his eyes halfway closed. When he saw there was no breakfast on the table yet, he went on another one of his tirades.

"What the hell you doin' Cali?! The last time I checked, you ain't Mama! "

I rolled my eyes and let out a slight groan. "She can't cook for us all the time, so here I am."

Brutus smacked his lips and said, "Fine. Just don't burn

anything, and hurry up! That bud I smoked last night is giving me the munchies like a mofo." He left the kitchen, sat down on the couch in the living room and changed the channel to *Yo! MTV Raps.* I was about to call him out on it when I heard Naughty by Nature's "O.P.P." playing, so I decided to give him a pass. When I was almost done cooking, Julius and Bolina both walked into the kitchen. Unlike Brutus, neither one questioned why I was cooking and patiently waited until I was finished.

"Breakfast is served everyone!" I called out. I was quite impressed with myself over how the spread turned out. I decided to add cheese to both the eggs and the grits. The fruit plate was fresh, colorful and highly pleasing to the eye. The sausage links were nice, hot and crispy and the flapjacks were soft, fluffy and well-browned, even if I couldn't make them a perfect circular shape.

"Not bad, Calliope. Not bad at all," Julius complimented, with Bolina and Isis nodding in agreement and Atum giving me a thumbs up.

"Eh, it's alright I guess," Brutus said condescendingly.

Julius turned to him angrily. "Well if that's the case, how come you cleaned your plate before everyone else did?"

"I got high last night, so I still got the munchies," Brutus snidely replied.

"Yo, ever since your punching bag got busted you've been using Cali as the replacement. You need to stop doing that and get a new one already!" Julius exclaimed.

Brutus and Julius started getting into it and all I could do was put my head into my hands and shake my head. This was the second morning in a row with an argument at the breakfast table. My family was falling apart right in front of my very own eyes.

"Hey! Can't we all just get along?" Atum quickly butted in to say. Brutus and Julius stopped arguing as we all turned to look at Atum, his face adorned with a cute smile. We were silent for a moment before my two older brothers cracked up, with me, Bolina and Isis following suit.

"Who up and made you Rodney King?" Bolina said amidst her giggles.

I was relieved at the moment of joy that just occurred. We all went back to eating breakfast as if the argument never happened. Isis, who was sitting the closest to the kitchen door, turned to look out the kitchen door and at the living room.

I noticed this and asked her, "Did something catch your eye?"

"It's Dad," she said anxiously. "He finally came home." We all looked towards the kitchen door and sure enough, she was right. Dad had returned, and with a guest. Walking behind him was Mr. Peloponnesian, in the flesh.

"Good morning family," he said to all of us with a grin, getting a glass to pour himself some orange juice as if nothing was suspicious. We all just continued to stare at him in silence. He finished pouring his glass, took a sip and asked us with a shrug of his shoulders, "Have I done something wrong?"

"Well, you made mama cry last night," Atum said to him with disdain.

"How could I have done that when I wasn't even here?" Dad asked with a laugh. Mr. Peloponnesian cleared his throat and nodded at dad for acknowledgement. "Oh, where are my manners? Family, I'd like you all to meet Zeu-se, the current patriarch of the House of Peloponnesian. To you all, he's to be addressed as Mr. Peloponnesian."

I took a closer look at Mr. Peloponnesian. He was just as tall and imposing as the pillars that adorned his house. He had ebony skin, a tightly curled, salt-and-pepper beard, a broad nose, jet black hair styled into a slicked back conk, and the darkest, meanest eyes I ever saw. Not even the half-smile on his face or the neatly tailored, light brown designer suit he was wearing could conceal them.

An air of unease and tension had accompanied his presence. Everyone in the room stared upon him in fear. I gulped before getting out of my seat in an attempt to diffuse the tension. I poured a glass of orange juice and offered it to him as a sign of hospitality, with a warm but shaky smile on my face.

"It's very nice to meet you, Mr. Peloponnesian," I said to him as I handed over the glass of orange juice.

"It's very nice to meet you as well, Calliope," he said with his deep, bass voice. I tensed up a little bit when he said my name. Being directly acknowledged caused me to feel nothing but intimidation.

"Well, it was nice to see all of you this morning, but me and Mr. Peloponnesian have some very important business matters to talk about. Hope all of you enjoy your day," Dad said to us. He and Mr. Peloponnesian then proceeded to make their way out of the kitchen. I saw them walk straight to the room at the other end of the living room hall and through the sliding door of the den, which sometimes served as Dad's bedroom whenever he and Mama had a really bad argument. I saw Mr. Peloponnesian light up a cigar as Dad, slid the door back into place so they could conduct their business in private.

"And to think you call me too nosy, Julius," I heard Bolina say jokingly. I turned around and realized that while I was investigating, everyone at the table had been silently staring at me the whole time.

"Oops," I said, tucking my hands behind my back and playing cute.

We all finished eating breakfast, washed our dishes and then went about our day. Julius and Bolina decided to spend a day in the Atlantic Colony. Brutus left to hang out with Perseus and his crew again, likely to smoke. Isis went to a friend's house and Atum went to Herc's house to hang out with his younger brother, Apollo. Knowing the only place I was allowed to go to by myself was the Garden of Artemis, I walked back up the staircase to get my notebook.

I noticed that the door to Mama's room was still closed. It was almost 10:00 AM and she still hadn't left her room yet, which was very unlike her. I thought about knocking on her door to see if she was okay but figured she probably wanted to be alone. I still wondered though, what was she so upset about? What had transpired when I was in homeschooling and down in the garden last afternoon?

I got my notebook, walked back down the staircase and before walking out the door, I took one more look at the door to the den. What were Dad and Mr. Peloponnesian talking about? What was his connection to our house?

As I made my way out of the door, it became clear to me that everyone had a door of their own. It was a most versatile device - one that could be used to protect any number of secrets and desires and not easily unlocked with a key.

Curiousity Kills The Cat

It was the first day of the summer of 1992. The smell of BBQ and the sound of g-funk filled the air. Kids were running around outside having the times of their lives. Families were having get-togethers. Summer love stories were sprouting out of the ground like daisies. I usually took it all in and would find some way to make a poem or story out of it, but not on this day. I felt distracted, uneasy and borderline disgusted. Learning that my warm, happy house was actually full of secrets had thrown everything off balance.

"Calliope!" Herc called out, surprising me with a tight hug from behind. I smiled as he took a seat next to me, before I sighed somberly and stared into the distance. Herc laughed a little bit in an attempt to lighten things up and I smiled briefly at him before looking away again.

Herc sighed. "What's eating you?"

"Nothing," I lied.

"Girl, I've known you long enough that I can tell when something's wrong with you. You know you can always tell me anything."

I looked back at my house in contemplation for a moment, before I sighed once more. "Apparently, my family members are bearers of secrets."

"Care to elaborate?"

"Well... yesterday my dad dropped this bombshell on us," I started before slightly choking up. "We're gonna be moving to Griffin. In two weeks."

"Hold up, y'all are moving? To Griffin?!" Herc asked in disbelief.

"I'm just as surprised as you are," I confirmed, "To make matters worse, he won't even tell us why."

Herc went silent and looked away before he turned back to me, nervously laughed and joked, "Do you think he has some sort of debt to the Griffin Mafia?"

"Herc, please don't!" I retorted before I softly punched him on the arm while he continued laughing.

"Look! It's Princess Calliope of Atalan and her royal prince, Herc!" Me and Herc both turned around and saw Atum and Herc's little brother, Apollo approaching us. Apollo was basically the spitting image of Herc, aside from the fact that he was much shorter.

I stood up and hugged both of them. "And how are you two little ones doing today?"

"As good as we can be with the two tyrants in our midst!" Atum said in a jokingly militant voice, to which I just smiled and shook my head.

"Well, what do our two neighborhood superheroes plan to do about that?" I asked playfully.

"I wanted to go into crimestopper mode, but Apollo doesn't seem so interested," Atum answered while Apollo shrugged with a smile.

I chuckled and told them, "Whatever you two do, make sure you keep the trouble at bay."

"Ah, will do, big sis! Laters," he replied, throwing up a peace sign before he and Apollo walked off. I saw that they were approaching Morpheus Avenue and couldn't help but let out a long sigh. It never ceased to frustrate me that even my youngest brother could venture more than I could.

"Is something wrong, Calliope?" Herc turned to me to ask.

"I'm just so tired of being a caged bird."

"Don't worry girl, it's just like your favorite song says: *one day you'll fly away, leave all this to yesterday!*" Herc sang.

"Herc! You are too silly sometimes!" I said, punching him softly on the arm again, happy he had said something to brighten my day yet again.

"You know, that was real cute right there. Your little bro callin' me a prince and you a princess, I mean."

I giggled. "Yes it was."

Herc looked away and, with a striking change in tone, said, "Sometimes, I wish it was true."

"Is that so?" I asked, my head tilted sideways, looking upon him with questioning eyes.

He lifted his head back up, put his hands behind his back, closed his eyes and played possum, as he answered, "Whoa there! No idea where all of that came from!"

"Uh-huh," I replied as I put my head back upright, while still giving him an inquisitive gaze.

"Come on now, girl! We're best friends! That would be weird!" Herc laughed awkwardly as his eyes showed unease.

"Yeah, I suppose so," I said with a frustrated sigh.

"Looks like it's that time again! Need to go help my pops out at the cleaners! Talk to you later, Cali!" He enthusiastically said as he stood up and walked out of the gazebo and towards Morpheus Ave.

"Same to you," I said in a deadpan manner. I could tell he was lying through his teeth. He'd told me time and time again how much he hated working with his dad at the cleaners. He only talked about going to work there with a grimace on his face and a groan in his voice. It was highly unusual for him to talk about it with such enthusiasm.

I looked towards Morpheus Avenue again. The yellow-green leaves of the trees that adorned the landscape served as shading for the many patios and balconies all along the avenue. Numerous characters walked up and down the sidewalk, in and out of the four or five dozen businesses that the street contained. A symbol of Auburn's affluence, the buildings all shared hues of golden browns and warm yellows, with neatly maintained 60s-era Cadillacs, 70s-era Rolls Royces and early 90s Jeeps in loud colors parked in front of them.

I wanted to see what desires that Herc was hiding from me. And the only way I could do so was if I had pushed down the arbitrary boundaries that had been set in place for me for all of my life. As this desire to disobey brewed within, it was then I looked back to my house. In one of the windows, I saw mom looking out at me. She smiled and waved, before I did the same. Once she walked away, I looked back to Morpheus Ave. and sighed, having been reminded that it wasn't so easy to push down the glass walls that surrounded my very being.

After spending another hour or so in the Garden of Artemis, continuing to write in my notebook, I went back home for the day. As I walked in, it felt as if everything had went back to normal. I could smell garlic, onions and tomato sauce cooking in the kitchen. I heard Smokey Robinson's voice on the record player. I made my way to the kitchen, only to see mom sitting at the breakfast table, sipping a cup of coffee while her lasagna was in the oven. I practically smashed into her for a hug.

"Mama! You're finally feeling better," I said enthusiastically.

"Oh yes, I'm feeling much better than I did yesterday. I had to check on the coffee shop and the shoe store today either way. Spending time at my businesses always makes me feel better; after all, they're the only things in my life I feel I have much of a hold on anymore," she said, sounding cheerful and anxious at the same time.

"What exactly do you mean by that?" I asked with my smile fading.

"You know Calliope, I promised you that I would tell you about what was wrong when I felt ready. I think now would be a good time for you to sit down," she said to me. I nodded my head and took the seat next to her.

"Did you see your dad this morning?"

"Yes, I did. And he was here with Mr. Peloponnesian too."

She took another sip of her coffee and said, "I know. They came together and left together. Your father is out and about doing god knows what, with god knows who."

"What do you think he's doing?"

"For a while, I've felt that he's been occupied with... well... other affairs," she leaned in towards me and said with a slight whisper, as if there were secret eyes and ears around us.

"What... kind of affairs?" I asked as my eyes grew even wider. I knew that my dad was keeping many secrets, but I had hoped that he at least didn't take it to the extent of infidelity.

"Well, first off, I believe that he has a cash flow or two on the side. I went to the office for his architecture firm the other day, and his business partners told me that they've been running the show for the past three months. They take care of the projects while your father always claims to be busy with something else."

"If he's not working his usual job, where is he getting money from?"

"It may seem a tad farfetched, but I think he and Mr. Peloponnesian are working with the mafia in Griffin. That's the thing about those Peloponnesians, they will stop at nothing to expand the extent of their business empire." Mama took another sip of coffee as she went on. "You always hear a little bit of something about everyone and everything on Morpheus Avenue. Lately, there's been talk that both the Peloponnesians and the Griffin Mafia are trying to make moves on South Atalan. This whole 'gentrification' thing they call it. If they're seeking to raise the rent, they're gonna need an architect, I suppose."

"It doesn't sound farfetched at all," I added. "The fact that Mr. Peloponnesian wants us to leave for Griffin so quickly is suspicious."

Mom shook her head in agreement. "That's true. I pretty much figured the same thing. I just don't know why your dad insists on working with Mr. Peloponnesian. One of his business partners is Mr. Peloponnesian's brother, Minos, but he renounced the Peloponnesian name long ago, so I doubt that he's in on it."

I pulled back slightly upon hearing that. In Atalan, to renounce the name of one's house meant to disown themselves from their family. And if they were unable to take any of the family fortune, they would be placed in a lower social class upon doing so. Usually that was only done in extreme cases, so I couldn't help but to wonder what happened within the walls of the House of Peloponnesian to cause Minos to sever ties with them. Having no idea how to react, I figured reassuring Mama was the best route to take.

"Well, at least it isn't a romantic affair he's been having," I said to her with a forced smile.

Mom went on to stare at me with unease before she closed her eyes and put her coffee cup down. I just stared at her as she went back to the oven and opened it, checking on the lasagna and garlic knots that were inside.

"Did I say something wrong?" I asked with a raised eyebrow, but she remained silent, focusing all of her attention on the contents of the oven until Dad walked in.

"Good evening everyone," he greeted as he nonchalantly walked into the kitchen.

"Good evening to you too, Pan. May I ask where you've been?" Mom asked him with a slight attitude while I looked on.

"Ah, I had a pretty eventful day today. We went to Griffin, and you two and the rest of the family are going to love our house out there."

Just hearing the name Griffin made me feel like I was stabbed in the heart, so I began to tune him out as he continued to tell Mama about our new house. It made me feel like everything dear to me was being taken away. The only house I had ever known. The Garden of Artemis. Herc. The view of the House of Peloponnesian. The red light.

While I could tell that he was going into detail over what awaited us out in Griffin, I felt too much at a loss to even care to listen. I didn't care about what awaited me in Griffin. Home is where the heart is, and my heart was in Auburn.

"Calliope?"

"Yes?" I asked, snapping out of my daze and turning to my mother.

"Go upstairs and tell your brothers and sister that dinner's ready," Mama said, taking the lasagna and garlic knots out of the oven.

"Will do, Mama." I got out of my seat and took a brief glance at Dad, who was sitting across the table with some papers. Whatever they were for didn't matter to me. I walked out of the kitchen towards the staircase as a whirlwind of thoughts swirled in my mind. The house I had spent my entire childhood in. The life I had always known. It was all to be gone. In less than one week.

II

Changes Begot Questions

Preparation

Demeter slowly nursed a cup of coffee as she sat in the back office of her shoe store on Morpheus Ave. Numerous papers were laid out in front of her, but all she could do was stare at them somberly.

"All of this hard work, only to be forced to sell off not one, but two successful businesses," she complained.

"Talking to yourself again?" she heard a voice ask. She looked up to see Urania, her friend and fellow business owner, standing at the door, shaking her head in a gray pantsuit. She was a tall, lanky woman with dark, musky skin, piercing hazel eyes and a short fro.

"Good morning to you too, Urania," Demeter greeted with a slight smugness. Urania laughed as she brushed her shoulder and sat down at the desk.

"So, what's the issue today? Is it Pan again?" she asked with a smug smile and a raised eyebrow.

Demeter shook her head and took another sip of coffee. "Urania, I need to know: is it easier being a lesbian?"

Urania laughed and shook her head. "Demeter, I'm not a lesbian! I've had relationships with both men and women!"

"But you were dating another woman for almost three years?"

"The length of time in each relationship doesn't matter! But to answer your question, we're all human. All relationships have problems, same sex or not." Urania explained.

Demeter scoffed. "I guess giving up men won't do me any good, huh?"

"Yeah, I can assure you that it won't!" Urania laughed, nodding her head for an unusual amount of time before uneasiness took over her eyes.

Demeter's face tensed in confusion. "What's the matter with you today?"

Urania closed her eyes and gulped before blurting out, "I have a message for you from Lady Hera."

"Lady Hera? What business is Miss Peloponnesian trying to sink her nose in now?" Demeter asked, her eyes glowering with annoyance.

"She wanted to let you know that, as of next week, she's going to be taking over both the shoe store and the coffee shop next door.

Demeter sat back and paused in disbelief for a moment before she yelled, "Motherfucker!"

"Now, now, Demeter, calm down. We both know you have trouble with... controlling your emotions. I don't want you to end up in a loony bin." Urania pleaded while holding her hands up.

"Calm down!? Oh, Urania, I'm fine! Just peachy!" she feigned, reaching into her drawer to pull out a flask of whiskey and mixing it in with her coffee.

As if in a sort of trance, Demeter began to stare off into space while drinking from her liquor-infused cup. Urania shook her head and, with concern in her eyes, got out of her seat and walked out of the office.

* * *

Herc laid in his bed, mulling over a daisy he picked from the Garden of Artemis. He let out a sigh as he began to pluck from it. "She loves me, she loves me not... she loves me... she loves me not... she... it don't matter anyway. Cuz she's leaving next week."

A tear began to roll down his cheek as he thought about Calliope, as he tearfully burst out, "How could I be so foolish? Why did I never tell her?"

He started to sob when there was a loud knock on the door, to which he shouted, "Who is it?"

"Answer your door and I'll tell you who it is, boy," his dad Leto said sternly from the other side.

Herc got up and made his way to the door. Leto was a stern man, with a bald head and thick, fuzzy mustache. His skin was a bistre tone, slightly lighter than Herc's. Tall and very imposing, he was a creature of little expression. Herc himself would even say that, while he knew that his father loved him very much, he had a very funny way of showing it.

"Yes?" Herc asked unenthused while scratching his neck.

"I just received another complaint about you from the Peloponnesians," Leto said, without so much as a shirk in his expression-less face.

"Again? What is it now?"

"Hermes said you spent too much time cleaning his room yesterday. Thinks you might have stole something."

"That's it? It don't help that ol' boy be havin' five or six girls in his room a night! Mystery fluid all over the place!" Herc exclaimed in disgust.

"I understand, but you really need to be more careful with

them. They have the power to override me and have you disowned from this house just like that," Leto said with a snap of his fingers.

Herc scoffed and said, "I wish they would."

* * *

On the ground level of the House of Peloponnesian, past the well-draped, golden ballroom where their famous soirees were held, Pan sat at the table in the drawing room. Decorated with portraits of past patriarchs and matriarchs of the House of Peloponnesian, with a large, silver chandelier hanging over the table, he was handed a cocktail by one of their maids. He took a sip and let out a sigh of refreshment before he looked back to Zeu-se across the long and shiny, mahogany wood table.

"So, Zeu-se, you still haven't explained just what purpose you have for me moving my house to Griffin?" Pan asked.

"We, the House of Peloponnesian, are forming a business alliance with the Griffin Mafia. You see, as we are the most powerful business empire of Central Atalan, and they are the most powerful business empire of Outer Atalan, it is a business decision which I regard as most wise. Being that you are one of my closest confidants, I'd like for you to be my eyes and ears out that way."

"I see," Pan replied with a chuckle, "I know you don't like for me to pry, but if you don't mind me asking, what exactly do you seek out of this alliance?"

Zeu-se took a sip of his cocktail. "A number of things. For starters, development, expansion and construction. Griffin has also surpassed the polis of Piedmont in terms of median family income and overall affluence. We here in Auburn are now on equal footing with them; only Savannah Beach and The Atlantic Colony surpass the two of us. However, our primary motivation is to secure territory."

Pan raised an eyebrow, took another sip of his cocktail and smiled as he said, "Secure the territory, huh?"

Zeu-se nodded. "To have Central Atalan involvement in an Outer Atalan polis would effectively leave South Atalan trapped. Griffin is just the first step, the next thing we need to do is get rid of the Clayton Syndicate, and then we'd have Clayton. After that, we need to get dispose of Magister Galene and take over Savannah Beach. Once those are under Central Atalan control, we can make the necessary moves to make South Atalan ours!"

"You're thinking of starting another Rupture?" Pan asked.

"If that's what needed, then so be it!" Pan and Zeu-se heard a voice gleefully shout from the doorway. It was there they were welcomed to the sight of a short, rounded woman with a hairdo akin to Farrah Fawcett.

"I'd assume that'd be no problem for a celebrated veteran of the Atalan Defense Forces," the woman said before she took a seat at the table.

"Well, well, about time you made it Narcissus," Zeu-se greeted, "Back in Atalan for good?"

Narcissus smiled and laughed, "Indeed, I am! Virginia Beach was a nice respite at first, but they're too tolerant a people for me. Apparently mermaids are really common around those parts. The gullible citizens of the place love to hang out at the beach all day just so they can get a glimpse of one. Idiots!"

"What a load of nonsense. They need to learn a thing or two from us over how to handle such freaks of nature," Pan scoffed.

The three of them all began to laugh, only for Narcissus to immediately stop and sternly ask, "So, Pan, how is baby Calliope doing?"

"Oh, she's far from a baby now. Just turned fifteen a few months ago, but everything's going well for the most part. As long as she does as she's told, we should have no problem," Pan answered.

"Good, good. Sounds like you've done well," Narcissus noted while nodding her head, "Perhaps a little bit of parole is in order then."

"What do you mean?" Pan asked with a raised eyebrow.

"I understand your house is moving to Griffin. The south-siders and Mystics know very well that they're not welcome there; you should have no problem keeping her docile and obedient. I think it's safe for you to allow her more freedom there. But she is to never set foot outside of the polis. It should be the perfect environment for her to have friends and attend school. As long as *you know what* remains out of her hands," Narcissus explained.

"Oh, but of course, Narcissus," Pan assured as the maid walked back into the drawing room. She just stood there to observe while Zeu-se glared at her.

"Hecuba! Don't just stand there! Prepare a drink for our guest!" Zeu-se demanded.

Hecuba nodded. "Yes sir."

Narcissus looked on at her as she walked to the kitchen, looking back to Zeu-se to say, "All these years and you still haven't fired her? That woman doesn't know the first thing about hospitality!"

Zeu-se laughed. "She's a good maid; she just doesn't like you. Still needs to remember she has a job to do though."

"Aww, she's still bitter about the A.D.F. killing her brother back in the 1970s," Narcissus said coyly while pouting her lower lip before she laughed, "Well that's too bad!"

"Good riddance!" Pan exclaimed, as the three of them then had another fit of laughter.

Narcissus then stopped and turned to Pan once more to say, "Well, Pan, I can honestly say I'm not too worried, but alas, we can't be too careful. We still have three more years before she turns eighteen, after all. To ensure that she stays in her place, I will be moving into the home next door to yours in Griffin. That way I can keep an eye on everything."

"That's fine by me. Not gonna lie, I do see glimmers of my sister's spirit within her from time to time, maybe your presence is what's needed to scare her off for good," Pan said.

"I'd love to do just that!" Narcissus enthused as Hecuba handed her a cocktail with a look of disdain on her face. Narcissus yanked it out of her hand before she took a sip, began to laugh as the three of them continued to talk more business.

$$* * *$$

It was there, in the Garden of Artemis, where I silently stood that day. Looking at the sunset in the distance. Interestingly, for a summer's eve, the park was completely empty. The time and air had a very odd feeling to it. I looked again to the window at the House of Peloponnesian. The curtains were unmoved. Oddly, I desired for the figure to peer out again. I wanted to know more. That was, until I heard a soft growl.

I turned around to see a wolf approaching me with brown, curly fur and eyes that almost looked human. He looked upon me knowingly as it paced in my direction. I gulped and backed away nervously. I took a step backwards for each step the wolf took forward, stumbling when he was right upon me. I began to shake and closed my eyes when I noticed the wolf was merely sniffing me.

"I am very glad to have found you, even if it required me to venture this far from the sacred domain," I heard a deep, baritone voice say from out of nowhere. I opened my eyes and looked around, only to see no one around me. Just the wolf, who still eyed me whilst nodding its head.

"Huh?" I thought to myself, when a dogcatcher truck had pulled up on the grass.

"There it is!" I heard one of the dogcatchers say as both of them walked out of the vehicle. The wolf just looked at them and, instead of running away, calmly allowed itself to get taken into the truck, but not before taking one more look back at me.

Once the wolf was placed in the truck, I heard one of the dogcatchers ask, "What is it with all of these wolves wandering out of the South Forest lately?"

"I have no idea," the other replied before they drove off. I began to stand myself up and brushed off the grass as I watched them drive away. I then walked over to the gazebo to ponder over what had just happened.

"Who was that talking earlier? Could it have been the wolf?" I asked myself before I shook my head and said, "Don't be ridiculous!"

I looked back at the House of Peloponnesian. The figure still hadn't peered out the window, and night had fallen. I couldn't make time go by any slower. I sighed once more as I walked back over to my house.

Moving Day

T he red light revolved the same way every night, signifying either a burgeoning excitement or an impending doom. Quivering and flickering like a flame, revolving around Atalan's nighttime sky as always, while everything in my room was packed into boxes. I tried to make the night longer. I tried to stare at the red light even closer. I squinted at the House of Peloponnesian until I started tearing up. I wrote until my hand hurt. None of it worked in the end.

I was mid-sentence in my writing when I dozed off. I woke up the next morning to everyone yelling my name.

I was beginning to stir when Julius barged into my room. "Calliope! Wake up already. It's moving day."

I pulled the covers off of myself, wiped my eyes with a yawn. "My stuff's already packed."

"Well, help us out a little bit downstairs will ya?" Julius asked before he left my doorway. I sat up, stretched my arms and yawned some more when I heard a rock hit my window.

"What the..." I said sleepily. I got up and looked out my window, only to see Herc in the yard with shrugged arms and a smile. I returned the smile and ran downstairs to go see him. Upon reaching the door, I saw that mom had already answered it.

"Hey, Calliope, Leto's boy wants to talk to you," she turned around and said to me. I gave her a slight nod of the head while I rushed past her to give Herc a ridiculously tight hug.

"Mama, is it okay if we speak on the porch for a minute?" I asked her. Mom raised her eyebrow for a moment, before she obliged. She closed the door and the two of us sat on the garden swing to talk.

"I'm really gonna miss you," Herc said to me with a melancholy tone in his voice.

"I'm gonna miss you more," I said with joyful sarcasm. I wanted to goof off with him at least one more time before I had to leave.

"Oh, you wanna make this a game, huh?" Herc said perkily.

"Maybe," I responded, playing along. We burst out into a loud fit of laughter until we got a whiff of BBQ in the park. It was then, I decided it was time to get back to packing.

"It's gonna be real weird not seeing you in the Garden, girl," Herc commented.

"It's gonna be real weird not being anywhere near you," I added.

"Well, til' the next time then," Herc said as he stood up and walked off the porch.

"Yeah, hopefully that will be sooner than later," I said to him. He turned to look back at me and smiled before going about his way. I watched him walk away and once he was out of view, I continued to sit on the garden swing for a few more minutes before going back into the house to help out with moving.

Mama was folding up the living room rugs. "Calliope, how do you know him?"

"He's my best friend. He's good people, Mama. Don't worry," I said to her.

She paused for a moment, with a blank stare on her face, before she lectured, "Calliope, it's good to hear you have a friend, but I'd prefer for it to be with someone of a higher social standing than his."

I found myself taken aback and deeply confused by her words. "What is that supposed to mean?"

She took a pause of her own, before she closed her eyes and shook her head. "Just do what's expected of you, my child."

Upon hearing those words come out of her mouth, I paused. My eyes furrowed into a furious glare as my blood boiled over like a hot pot of tea.

"You know what? I'm sick of living like this, Mama! When will I be allowed to live my own life? Please tell me!" I exclaimed.

"Baby, you just don't understand," she said, reaching over to pat me on the shoulder.

"When will I ever understand!?"

"There will come a time when I will tell you, but now is not that time."

"Wow! And you wanna talk about Dad having too many secrets? Well, you're no different!" I yelled, storming past some of the movers carrying a wardrobe down the stairs. Isis and Atum were both in the hallway carrying boxes of stuff from their rooms and I was so livid that I almost pushed them over. All I could focus on was getting to my room. Upon reaching it, I slammed the door, and with my bed still there amidst the many boxes, I kneeled down on it and started to cry my soul out.

"How dare her? HOW DARE HER?!" I shouted between sobs. I cried for a few minutes before I heard a knock on my door.

"Go away!" I yelled.

"I'm not gonna go away," Brutus said, opening the door and stepping inside.

"Look Brutus, I am in no mood for any of your obnoxious jeers or rude remarks! Leave me alone!" I yelled at him with my face still in my arms.

"I actually came up because I was worried about you," he said in the softest, sweetest tone I had ever heard him speak with. I took my face out of my arms, my eyes still red from the tears and took a look at him. His usually scowled eyes had softened as he softly smacked his lips, eyeing me with concern.

"Oh, now you wanna be a good brother?" I asked him cynically.

He sat down on my bed and held me tight. "Okay, I know I'm an asshole and the two of us have definitely had our differences. But at the end of the day, you're my little sister. I'm not gonna just ignore it when I see you hurting."

My sobs were immediately halted by my shock. *Who was this guy and what had he done with the Brutus I had known all my life?*

My mouth stood agape for a few seconds. "Thanks, Brutus," I mustered out. "Thanks for caring."

"Anytime," he said softly, hugging me a little tighter. He even gave me a kiss on the forehead before getting off my bed and walking out of my room. Was that the real him? Or was it part of some elaborate practical joke he was about to pull off? Either way, I appreciated the moment of kindness, enough so that it motivated me to finish packing.

Several hours passed and night fell. The movers had dismantled my bed and placed it in their truck. In mere minutes, it would be time to leave Auburn and the original House of Thessaly, forever. I just stood in my empty, darkened room and looked around for a moment, before the window caught my eye. I walked towards it and perched myself on the window sill. I slowly extended my arm in the direction of the red light. It appeared to revolve slower than usual that night, as if it was sad I was going away.

"Calliope! It's time to go!" I heard mom call from downstairs.

I let out a long sigh, closed the window and made my way down the stairs. Save for the living room, the entire house was empty and shrouded in darkness. Seeing my childhood home that way was the most eerie feeling. The curtain-less windows seemed to droop down like the face of sad child. The doors creaked and made mild swings back and forth, wishing for attention. I ran my hands across the cold living room wall, to let the house know that I wasn't abandoning it. Not in my heart at least. I could feel the wall warm up slightly when it received my message.

"Calliope, stop messing around, we're ready to go," Mom called as she stood in the hallway that led from the living room to the carport.

"Okay Mama," I said breathily. She walked back to the carport, while I made sure to blow the wall a kiss before leaving, just to let the house know that someone loved it.

I walked through the glass doors that led to the carport, turning to take one final look at the courtyard and pool garden. I let out another sigh as I observed the pool's tranquil, turquoise glow, illuminating the statues and plants that surrounded it. As Dad pulled off from under the arches of the carport in his golden Cadillac Deville with Julius and Brutus, mom loudly honked the horn of her dark blue Silver Spirit-model Rolls Royce, with Isis and Atum sitting inside. I quickened my pace to get in her car, rolling my eyes at how rude and impatient she was being.

"Calliope, what has been with you today?" Mom angrily inquired when I sat in her car.

"Nothing," I answered snidely. Mom scoffed, showing that she didn't believe me. I stared out the window in silence as she pulled out of the carport. Although I kept my calm demeanor, I could feel a slight tear trickle down my face as we began to drive off. We were actually leaving our home. I couldn't believe it.

I became so overwhelmed with sadness that I had to look away. As we drove around the loop and out of the cobblestone driveway, I gazed at the Garden of Artemis and the House of Peloponnesian. All seemed to be normal with the nighttime lovebirds and kids staying out too late, all while the House of Peloponnesian sat undisturbed, resting up for its next party.

I looked closer at the balconies that faced the Garden of Artemis and noticed a figure standing on the one where I spotted someone peeking out of the window the week prior. It appeared to be a tall boy, but I couldn't make out anything else about him in the darkness that shrouded the figure.

Just as I had always reached out to the red light, this figure appeared to be reaching out in our direction. I wondered why he was reaching out towards us. Or maybe he was specifically reaching out towards me? Was it Adonis? I looked away to contemplate the sight for a moment. As this thought rolled through my mind, I looked back to see the figure. And just as quickly as the red light was pulling away, the figure was gone, transitioning back into the dark shroud of moss that had covered the balcony.

Dysfunction

e were all silent for the first couple of miles on our way to Griffin, retreating into our own worlds as we reached the grand Piedmont Bridge, the link between the island of Central Atalan and the peninsula of Southern Atalan across the bay. Covered with dazzling gold arches and massive, gold light pillars at each quarter mile interval, it was one of the most impressive sights one could ever see. It was my first time seeing it since I was a child, but I was still too fixated on the figure from the Peloponnesian house balcony to be excited about it.

As we drove down the Piedmont Bridge, Atum loudly bursted out, "I am not feeling the love in this car!"

Isis giggled a little bit, but I remained still, silently looking over the bay. I appreciated Atum trying to lighten things up, but at that moment, I simply wasn't feeling it.

"You're exactly right, Atum. Everyone's acting very distant, especially you, Calliope," Mom said irritably.

"What are you talking about, Mama?" I asked back sarcastically.

"See, that's what I mean! There's no need for this passive-aggressiveness."

"You're not even making sense! If I want to be alone with my thoughts, then let me be!"

"You're acting a lot like your father right now. Just sitting there, upset about something and not even trying to talk about it. You can trust me, Calliope. There's no need to be secretive."

"I'll stop when you stop being secretive with me!" I yelled at her while crossing my arms.

"I already told you baby, now's not the time for you to know," Mom replied with a softer tone in her voice. I groaned and turned back to the window. We had just about finished crossing the bridge at that point and were now entering Inman. It was nicknamed the Five Points because when entering the area from the Piedmont Bridge, the streets diverged away from the bridge like a star, with two streets heading directly east and west, another two streets heading southeast and southwest and the main street, Aglaea Avenue, heading directly south. The knots I felt inside of me eased up as we entered the area.

"Could you guys stop? Everyone's been fighting lately and I'm tired of it," Isis coaxed. I turned to Isis, smiled, and gave her a hug to comfort her.

Mama sighed. "I'm sorry you and Atum had to see that. Calliope and I really should have held our tongues until we were alone."

"I think you mean *you* should have held your tongue," I responded to her cynically.

"Oh, now I know you know better than to disrespect your own mother like that, Calliope!" Mama bit back, scowling at me in the rearview mirror.

"Please don't get started again," Isis said while holding her forehead.

Mom just sighed and went on, "Well, since Calliope always talks about how she never gets out, and the two of you have never been south of the Piedmont Bridge, maybe now would be a nice time to give the three of you a little tour. This right here is the heart of Inman, or the Five Points. I used to spend a lot of time here during my wilder college days."

As she was talking, I looked out the window at Aglaea Avenue, already having grown fond of the area. Architecturally speaking, there was no rhyme or reason for the buildings, with purple Victorian houses next to brown Dutch Colonial houses.

There were an innumerable amount of buskers, some singing, some reciting poetry. There was even a duo who had made makeshift drums out of garbage cans and boxes, loudly playing away. There was a group of girls dressed in ripped jeans and studded vests with crazy hair colors. In front of the jazz lounge, stood an older man in a fedora, coolly smoking a cigarillo. Across the street was a younger man with locs down to his waist, standing in front of the head shop.

Why can't we move here instead? I thought to myself as I took in all the sights.

"This right here is the Druid Highlands," Mama said, as our drive transitioned into the next polis. I looked out the window and saw a hilly landscape of large, nondescript brick buildings, many of which appeared to expel gas, smoke and other possibly toxic materials out of their rooftops as the center of industry and manufacturing in Atalan.

We made a turn onto another street, bookended by an elaborate, brown-painted arch with a tiled, pointed roof. I was taken aback at how none of the signs on the buildings and businesses on this street were in English. We drove past numerous restaurants, businesses and even an open-air market as the street was almost unanimously populated with people of Asian descent.

At the end of this street, there were six large movie screens that formed a large circle, with a long line of cars leading towards a gate with a sign that said Thebes Drive-In and a marquee advertising *Batman Returns, Sister Act, Patriot Games, Alien 3, Encino Man* and *Lethal Weapon 3.* I looked on with excitement, but before I knew it, we made another turn down a steadily sloping street with pillars in the middle that held up the train tracks for one of the lines of the Atalan Subway. I felt another lump in my throat as our car drove even further down the slope. It felt like Auburn was farther than ever. As we turned around a curve in the street, I looked back up to see Thebes Drive-In with the colorful lights of the Five Points and the Piedmont's bridge glowing even further in the distance as it all pulled away.

"If your windows are down, make sure you roll them up right now. We're about to enter the Cascade," Mom warned. I took another look out my window and saw abandoned buildings with crude graffiti tags scribbled all over them. several of the surrounding streets appearing to be bathed in complete darkness. Several of the surrounding streets were bathed in complete darkness as most of the street lights emitted a dim, yellow glow while a number of them didn't seem to be working. We drove by a small pack of men who were talking on the sidewalk, and just as we passed them, the group broke into a brawl.

Although I was initially terrified, I continued to observe the neighborhood and started to feel a sense of warmth and attachment. It was truly the oddest sensation. As we drove past the train station, curiously named Downtown Meleagea, I felt an immediate urge to look down one of the streets, only to bear witness to this lime-green building decorated in Christmas lights that was several blocks away. It was there where I felt the strongest connection of all. These buildings I've never seen before. These people I've never met. And yet, somehow, I'm connected to them.

"Tell us more about this neighborhood, Mama," I inquired.

"All you need to know is that you must never come here!" Mom exclaimed hurriedly, as the car picked up speed.

As the already dimly lit Cascade pulled away, we reached a highway underneath a tunnel. The brick arches that adorned the sides of the tunnel revealed a forested area, bathed in complete darkness. I heard the loud rumble of the Atalan subway over our heads, giving way to hollering, cheers and loud music. I looked out the window and through a translucent mist of steam, I saw the Mykonos Hot Springs. A mating ground for wild and active youths, I could feel a warm calm come over me as we drove through the hot spring mist. So calming that before I knew it, I had dozed off.

"Calliope?"

I looked around, but all I could make out were street lights as I turned to my window. Mama opened the door, softly patting me on the shoulder to wake up.

"Wake up, Calliope. We've just made it to Griffin."

The Box

A cobblestone path led to an elaborate beige and gold two-toned arch over the double-doored entrance to the house. Most of the architecture in Griffin was a testament to Southern Italy during the Renaissance, with tile roofs, soft, curved arches adorning doors, windows and pathways, large round domes and imposing towers. Our house in particular had a three-story tower, off-center from the entrance of the house, the third floor being a large suite which was used as an interior guesthouse. It also had a color scheme of beige, gold and olive brown which resonated throughout with red and purple shutters that featured yellow star and crescent moon patterns all over them that adorned the windows. The roof was flat and doubled as a large balcony. I felt sure I would be able to see the red light and the Atalan skyline from there.

We were all as distant as ever as we walked into the house. Dad told us where our rooms were and that the movers had already placed our stuff in them and that was the last word anyone uttered that night. Beautiful as it was on the outside, I already didn't like this house. A freezing cold wind blew away the warmth I once felt. Open doors were now shut, while love had been eclipsed by secrets.

I walked up the stairs, only to see a dimly-lit hallway with all of the doors closed. My room was the second room to the left. I walked in and promptly shut my door, since it appeared to be the new trend. I began to unpack my stuff and started decorating my room with the curtains, sheets and drapes all swaddled in rich reds. I hung up posters of people I admired like The Fresh Prince and Janet Jackson while I organized my large collection of stuffed animals and figurines of various cartoon characters.

Finishing up my room, I noticed a small, dusty box I didn't remember packing. I picked it up, letting out a loud sneeze as the dust popped out of it like a jack in the box. I turned away for a moment to gasp for fresh air while waving away the dust particles before I looked back into the box to see what it contained.

Inside was a mahogany wood box, shaped like a treasure chest. The lid was adorned with an engraving of a heart with a knife going straight through it. Already curious enough, I pulled the box out and lightly blew at it to remove the excess dust. Upon closer inspection, I saw a golden lock next to an engraving of the name: *Calliope.* I put the box down and just stared at it for a moment. It had my name engraved on it, but was too old and dusty to have been a gift.

It was locked tight, so I reluctantly stuck my hand back into the dusty old box it came from to see if there was a key inside. I turned away due to the dust particles still swirling around as I felt around for a key. I felt a skip in my heart from excitement when my hand brushed against it, only to hear a knock at the door.

"Calliope?" I heard Julius say.

I hurriedly put the box and key back into its package and slid it under my bed before I answered, "Come in."

Julius walked in with a soft smile on his face and tone in his voice, asked me, "Everything alright with you? I know you were a little upset earlier."

"Yeah, I'm feeling much better now. I was just upset about not being able to see Herc for a while," I answered with a lump in my throat.

"I'm really happy to hear that, little sis," Julius said with a nod, "See you at breakfast tomorrow."

"Good night Julius. I appreciate you checking up on me," I said. He softly nodded his head with a smile before closing my bedroom door. After he left, I pulled the box back out from under the bed. I took the box out of the package, along with its key. Butterflies sped around like racecars within my stomach as I slid the golden key into the lock and opened the box. Upon hearing the lock click, the butterflies accelerated in speed. I had joy in my eyes and a smile across my face for the first time since that morning, excited to see what the box contained.

The inside of the box was lined with a red-violet velvet cushion and contained many notes and folded pieces of paper, on top of various trinkets, including sweet-smelling incense cones, a rosary that looked like a dwarfed version of the Sistine Chapel and two large, golden hoop earrings, with an interwoven ribbon design. As I dug through the contents of this box, I discovered an old book buried underneath all of it. The book's cover bore nothing but a gold inscription in cursive which read "Calliope" against a solid, crimson backdrop.

I froze in place as I looked upon the book, confused and a little frightened. My room began to feel strangely cold as I held the book. A sudden, freezing wind passed through, even though the door and the window was sealed tight. I didn't know what to make of any of it. There was a sense of wonder with an equal sense of unease and also a little fear.

I gazed down upon the box's contents once more, closing in on the various notes littered about. I couldn't help but to wonder what stories and secrets they told. I briefly looked over my shoulder, as if I thought someone were watching me, before I picked up one of the folded red pieces of paper.

"*April 9th, 1973*

It's times like these where I wish I had never been born. I was just fired from my job at the library today for setting one of the patrons on fire—"

I took a pause to let it sink in. This other Calliope was the type of person who would set someone on fire? I looked away from the note before I continued to read nervously.

"*Even by Auburn standards, this patron was fairly pompous and stuck-up. He showed me nothing but blatant disrespect and condescension as I showed him around the library and, after five minutes of that nonsense, I just couldn't take it anymore, so I recklessly conjured a ball of fire and threw it at him. Thankfully, no one but him saw me throw the ball of fire, and I quickly found a fire extinguisher to douse him out, but the damage was already done. Although the librarian initially took my side, word of the event was spread around quickly enough that Auburn's soothsayer made her way down to the library herself and forced her to fire me due to suspicious actions.*

The Oracle told me about keeping my emotions in check, lest I lose control of my abilities, and yet I failed to do that. Lord knows what would have happened had I been caught by a Magister or a member of the Atalan Council. We're on the heels of the 1972 Rupture, so things are tense right now. Having been yelled at by my dad and chided by my brothers after this happened, I ran away from home again to stay with my friends Urania and Moneta in Inman. How long it will be before I return, I don't know, but I do know that I need some help in keeping this all in check. Both the emotions, and the powers.

"Well that was... odd," I pondered, placing the paper back in the box. I looked back at the box curiously, before I decided to shut the box and go to sleep for the night. Upon closing it, I saw both of my hands emit a faint light. It was only for a few seconds, but I still gasped at the sight and quickly placed one of my hands to my face. I waved it around, but the light was already gone, and I couldn't do anything to bring it back.

My eyes tensed up and I asked myself, "What's going on?"

Unsavory Dealings

"Your gift is returning, baby Calliope. No doubt it will awaken soon."

"Huh!? Who was that!?" I shouted out as I pried my eyes open and quickly sat up in my bed. I took a look around my room, wondering where the soft, ethereal feminine voice I had heard could be coming from. My eyes nervously bolted around the room, before they rested upon the box. I raised my eyebrow; pondering if the box was somehow speaking to me.

"Open the box," I heard the voice say to me once more.

"Huh?" I asked as I looked up and around my room, "Who and where are you?"

"The Realm of The Spirits is a most intricate place," the voice laughed. *"Just know that I am someone very important to you, Calliope. Now, go and open the box."*

I nodded hesitantly and made my way to the box. Upon opening it, I found a folded red note sitting curiously on top of everything. I stared at it wide-eyed as I didn't remember leaving any of the folded pieces of paper on top. The note was practically begging to be read, so I unfolded it.

"August 14, 1975

Earlier today, I woke up to the feeling of various aches all over my body and the sound of Pleione yelling at her boyfriend. As I looked on, the argument became progressively louder and more intense before

Cleon walked in the room to break it up. Her boyfriend just threw his hands up and left the room before I asked Cleon and Pleione what was going on. After all, I had no memory of the night prior nor any idea what I was doing in her bed. They both just stared at me nervously before explaining that they had to save me from the Griffin Mafia.

The last thing I remembered was walking down Penia Street, only to come face to face with a man in a suit who claimed to be from the dreaded House of Caligula. It was then he gazed deeply into my eyes and tried to use mind control to trick me into spilling the beans on the hideout for the Atalan Resistance. The Oracle already told me all about the malevolent wielders of this ability, and taught me a handy trick to use in case I need to resist it. Alas, it was of no use; he was exceptionally powerful in his skill. He forcefully shoved my face into his pried my eyes open, when I finally succumbed.

Apparently, he began to beat me severely, with several other members of the Mafia emerging to take part when Cleon and some of the other Lords promptly intervened and shooed them away. Pleione in turn insisted that I be brought back to their place for safe keeping. Grateful as I am that they were around to save my life, I can't help but to feel a bit embarrassed. The Oracle and many other members of our Coterie go on about how powerful I am, and yet I couldn't even successfully resist mind control.

I also felt bad for Pleione. Given that her boyfriend is from a Mafia family, her paranoia about his possible involvement is through the roof, even though Cleon and I both know better. I don't know her boyfriend very well, I can't even remember his name, but aside from a bit of an attitude problem, he's a good guy. Alas, The Cascade has a history with Griffin. No one seems to know the whole truth, but what's known for sure is that the two don't trust each other.

Which begs the question......what were they doing wandering

around in a neighborhood where they weren't wanted? Surely, they aren't seeking to start another Rupture, are they?"

My eyes grew wide before I gulped as I refolded the note and placed it back in the box. I already felt uneasy at the thought of being in the presence of the Griffin Mafia, so to read about some of their past crimes definitely didn't help. Furthermore, the note had brought even more questions to the table for me.

I looked up to the ceiling and nervously asked, "Um, hey, whoever you are, do you have any idea what this girl is talking about? Like what are these tricks and powers?"

There was a moment of silence, as I steadily looked around the room, only to flinch once the mysterious voice answered, *"Just keep reading the box. You will find out in due time."*

$$* * *$$

As the morning broke in, Julius stepped out onto the balcony to his room. The balcony overlooked the round, fountain-adorned pool to the new House of Thessaly. It should have seemed like the life to live in a house so grand in size, whimsical in its execution and topped off with a simple yet elegant pool. And yet, all Julius could think about was Bolina as a tear began to stream down his face as he looked down into the pool.

"Man, what's eatin' you now?" Brutus asked loudly after bursting into Julius's room.

"Brutus?! Man, is sensitivity a foreign language to you or what!?" Julius retorted.

Brutus laughed. "Well shit, I'm asking you what's wrong. That ain't sensitive enough for you?"

Julius scoffed and answered, "I was forced to break up with my girl last night. I don't see how that could be funny to you."

In his shirtless, potbellied glory, Brutus walked up to Julius with a smile and slapped him on the back. "There's a million more fish in the sea out there, and you haven't even reached your peak yet. You could go out and get another girl just like that, but instead you over here in your room cryin' over a high school sweetheart!"

Julius held his head down before saying, "Yeah, I'm crying over Bolina. She was the girl I wanted to marry. If you knew what love was, you'd understand. But what am I saying? You don't even know how to show love to your own family."

"Is that so? Cuz last I checked, I was the one who gave Cali a shoulder to cry on after she got into that argument with moms yesterday," Brutus began with a facetious grin. "Where was you? Oh yeah, that's right, getting in one last quickie at the park! "

Julius held his head back up, scowled his eyes, and retorted, "Excuse me, bro? Love ain't some type of game, man! At least I'm always nice to Calliope. You on the other hand treat her like she don't even belong in the family!"

Brutus laughed. "You're trying to tell me she does?"

"Will the two of you quit actin' like little fools and come downstairs? Me and your mother need you," Pan said in a calm, assertive manner as he walked into the door to Julius's room.

"Yeah, Julius!" Brutus exclaimed sarcastically, much to Julius's annoyance.

* * *

"Well, this is it!" Mom said enthusiastically as she stepped out of the car with her arms wide open. Julius, Brutus and I all stepped out of the car to look up at her new business space before

I took an observant glance at the street we were on. Ponos Street was Griffin's main thoroughfare. The buildings were fanciful, Italianate creations which wouldn't have been out of place in Naples, but all I could focus on was how strangely it lacked color compared to the other parts of Atalan. The four of us stuck out like weeds in a rose garden. The stares we were getting from onlookers weren't helping me feel any more welcome.

"Calliope, will you pay attention?" Mom asked with a curt tone, snapping me out of my daze. "This is where my new bakery and cafe will be! And I would like for you, Julius and Brutus to help out."

"What if I don't wanna help out?" Brutus asked.

"You don't have a choice for now! I don't know anyone in Griffin yet and I can't do it all by myself!" Mom exclaimed. I just rolled my eyes at the exchange. She was getting more ornery by the minute and Brutus had returned to his usual obnoxious, smartass self.

"You can always rely on me for help," I heard a man who sounded like Robert de Niro say. The four of us turned around and saw a short, bald man, with light olive skin and a chubby build, walking towards us, wearing sunglasses and smoking a cigar. He took a puff before he tilted his sunglasses, revealing his hazel eyes, and extended his hand towards mom for a handshake.

"The name's Romulus, at your service," he said.

Mom hesitantly returned the handshake and said, "Hello there, I'm Demeter. May I ask who you are and why I should rely on you for help?"

Romulus took another puff of his cigar. "Let's just say I'm a businessman in the area. As for why you should rely on me for help, I helped your husband get his hands on the lease for this storefront. If he can rely on me, then you should have no problem, Mrs. Thessaly."

"Mafia," I muttered with an eye roll, observing the exchange.

"Then tell me why I've never even heard of you?" Mom stiffly asked.

Romulus took another puff of his cigar as he raised his left eyebrow before he responded, "Funny, I assume it's the husband's job to tell his wife everything."

"I would think so too, but that's not the case in my marriage."

"Well, I'm here to offer you my assistance in getting this place off the ground! My brother Cicero has some supplies for you stocked up in his pizza shop across the street."

"Well then, it's nice to know that some money is going to stay in my pocket after all. Come on babies, it's time to get to work!"

Julius and Brutus followed Romulus to grab the supplies from the pizza shop while I went inside the cafe with mom. As she held the door open, she looked at me with a smile and said, "Aren't you excited, Calliope?"

I returned the smile and answered, "Yes, yes I am." In all honesty, I only said that to avoid another argument with her. I felt like I was surrounded by more secrets than ever, especially after the confirmation that my father had been working with the Griffin Mafia after all. Suffice to say, I wasn't feeling particularly thrilled about anything that morning.

Something Like A Business

"Today's the day! The Cornucopia Bakery & Cafe will finally be open for business!" Mom shouted enthusiastically while I set up the decorations on the service counter. I smirked a little when I saw how optimistic she was. I was happy that my mother was happy again. As for me, I was merely just content. Laying out green and red bamboo placemats, organizing the fake fruits in the woven, wicker basket cornucopia on display at the end of the counter closest to the entrance and making chalk drawings of coffee pots and croissants on the menu were all a means of keeping my mind off of everything else.

Mama's smile looked more and more fake every day, while Dad remained as distant and secretive as ever. He rarely even showed up at the breakfast or dinner table anymore. My siblings all grew more and more reclusive by the day. The warmth I used to feel within Julius's presence had been replaced by emptiness. Isis's smile slowly waned away. Atum had either run out of material or given up the comedy thing. Even Brutus became quiet and reserved, and strange as it was, I actually missed his loud mouth and obnoxious behavior.

I wanted my family to go back to the way they were. I wanted to go back to our old house. I wanted to see Herc again. I wanted to spend time in the Garden of Artemis, laying in the grass and writing away until the sun had set and the red light began.

"Hey Calliope! Hurry up with that espresso, will ya!?"

"Okay Cicero, just a minute!" I exclaimed as I checked to see if the espresso was finished brewing.

"How does Pan do it? If she was my daughter, she'd be on the curb by now with an attitude like that," Cicero complained to Romulus in the loudest whisper I ever heard. I rolled my eyes and finished topping off his espresso with the crema. I gave it one last stir before I walked out to his table.

"Well, it's about time," he said, taking a puff of his cigar before yanking the espresso out of my hands. Cicero was considerably taller than his brother Romulus, despite being several years younger. Like Romulus, his head was also bald, but his skin was somewhat paler, and he had green eyes, a brown goatee and a much larger physique.

"Glad to know my service is appreciated," I said to him in a deadpan, sarcastic manner.

Romulus took another puff of his cigar and laughed while Cicero stared at me blankly before retorting with, "Your ma over there really needs to teach you a thing or two about common courtesy, young lady."

"Well, if you want respect, then you should probably give some respect beforehand don't you th-"

"Excuse my sister, fellas!" Brutus said, cutting me off in the middle of my comeback, frantically pulling me away to the kitchen.

"What was you thinkin' Calliope!? That's the Griffin Mafia right there!" Brutus fearfully whispered.

"So?" I calmly replied, shrugging my shoulders.

"*So?!* They're the last people you wanna try and tell off!

Cicero's probably got a body bag with your name on it by now after you just dissed him like that!"

"And you're the last person to try and tell anyone they need to have more tact, Brutus. Now excuse me," I walked out of the kitchen and sat at one of the tables on the patio for a quick breather. I closed my eyes before proceeding to stretch my arms and exhale.

"My dad's an asshole, isn't he?" I heard a girl say.

I opened my eyes and looked at the table next to me only to see a girl with long, straight black hair, big lips and big, brown eyes. Like Romulus and Cicero, her skin was olive, but much darker in tone. An oversized, blue flannel shirt adorned her stick-thin figure as she took a drag of her cigarette.

"The name's Fortuna, would you like a smoke?" she said as she motioned her pack of cigarettes towards me.

I smiled and asked, "What kind are they?"

"Newports," she answered.

"Sure," I said, reaching over and taking a cigarette from her. "I used to smoke these with my friend back in Auburn."

Fortuna laughed and said, "You're Calliope, right?"

I nodded and answered, "Yep, that's me."

"Well, just so you know, when my dad gets like that, just ignore him. As big and scary as he tries to be, he's mostly just talk."

"Yeah, I can tell," I said before the two of us started laughing. Fortuna then paused to stare at me for a moment before she smiled.

"I sense really good energy from you. That's rare around these parts," she noted cryptically.

"Um, gee, thanks, I guess?" I said with a chuckle, to which she joined in.

"Don't worry, I hate it around here too," Fortuna added.

"And... how did you know that?" I asked in confusion.

"Let's just say I have my ways," Fortuna shrugged with a laugh.

I just shrugged back. "Glad I'm not the only one!"

"Yeah, you definitely aren't," Fortuna laughed, "You guys are from Auburn, right? It must really suck having to leave the island for a gold-covered shithole like this place."

"I really do miss it," I sighed. "I miss being able to perch my arms on my window sill each night just to look at the radiant, nighttime glow of the Atlantic Colony."

Fortuna's mouth dropped and her eyes widened before she exclaimed, "I am SO jealous! The only thing I ever had to look at from my bedroom window was that stupid forest! I would have loved to see the hustle and bustle, not a bunch of trees being fertilized by the rotting corpses of Griffin Mafia victims!"

"I believe it," I said before I looked away and sighed. As I continued to nurse my cigarette while nonchalantly looking at the street, out of the corner of my eye I spotted Fortuna staring at me, her doe-like eyes radiating with sympathy and concern.

Fortuna, in a much softer voice, began, "Okay, look, I wasn't going to try to warn you or say anything at first. To me, if someone chooses to start working with the Mafia, then they totally deserve it when shit hits the fan. But you're different. I can tell that you're a good person who didn't want any part of this."

As I finished up my cigarette, I looked to her to ask, "What are you getting at?"

Fortuna looked away and sighed before she went on, "Just.....just be careful, Calliope. Keep a low profile, and if your parents get pulled in any deeper, then that's the time to run. Trust me on this."

I felt goosebumps before I gulped and hesitantly said, "Okay, well, thanks for the warning."

"Not a problem. I've known too many victims throughout my entire life, I don't want to see another one," Fortuna said ominously, "You'll probably see me bumming around Ponos Street and Pompeii Square a lot, since its summer. Don't be afraid to stop by and say hi."

"Oh, of course," I chuckled, "I gotta get back to work. It was nice talking to you, Fortuna."

"Same," Fortuna said as I walked back into The Cornucopia. It felt good to have someone to call an acquaintance.

The hours whizzed by as I served coffee and pastries to customers. Julius manned the stove and the oven with top speed while Brutus took the orders and mom greeted and made chit-chat with everyone. After a while, I barely noticed Romulus and Cicero were still there.

After three or four hours of working non-stop, I made a mocha macchiato, sat down at one of the tables and took a quick break. As I was nursing my coffee, two middle aged ladies walked in, gossiping and giggling like they didn't have a care in the world.

One of them looked like a mom straight out of a 1950's sitcom, in a green and white checkered dress that was well-fitted on her upper body but blossomed out like a flower from her waist to her knees. The other woman was slightly taller and curvier, with long, brown hair worn in cascading waves, a full face of makeup and dressed head to toe in designer labels such as Prada and Chanel. The two ladies stopped and looked over the selection of pastries in the glass display at the counter.

"Good afternoon and welcome to The Cornucopia! How may I assist you two lovely ladies?" Brutus enthusiastically greeted.

They both looked up from the display and appeared to flinch when they saw him at the counter. The fashionista's startled eyes and open mouth were a clear display of how confused and uncomfortable she was. The sitcom mom gulped and clutched her purse a little bit tighter, despite the fact there was no possible way for Brutus to grab it.

Brutus raised his eyebrows and asked, "Is everything okay?"

"Oh, we're fine! We're just a little shocked to see a business owned by people of a different, well, um, background around here, that's all," the fashionista said as I took another sip of my coffee.

"And what's that supposed to mean?" I butted in.

"Yeah!" Brutus added before he went on to scowl at them.

"Ladies, excuse my kids! They still have a thing or two to learn about customer service!" Mama shouted as she swooped in from her office, briefly side-eyeing us before she went on to smile at the two ladies.

The sitcom mom nodded. "Yes, I can see that." I rolled my eyes and went back to sipping my coffee.

Mom took over the cash register from Brutus and she extended her hand towards them. "Well, my name is Demeter."

The fashionista returned the handshake and responded, "Pleasure to meet you, Demeter. My name is Hestia and this lovely lady next to me is my good friend Themis."

"It's a pleasure, Demeter," Themis said before offering her a handshake. Mama began taking their orders as Brutus and Julius came to sit at the table with me.

"I knew we was gonna meet some uppity, Stepford types sooner or later," Julius muttered while Brutus was shaking his head.

"Tell me about it," I said, observing Mama chatting with them, looking like a bunch of gossipy old hens.

"Calliope, I need you to make two lattes and warm up an almond croissant and a banana nut muffin for our two guests here," Mama ordered.

"Got it," I replied, returning to the kitchen. Themis and Hestia sat at a table with Mama joining them shortly afterward. After serving them their coffees and pastries I returned to the kitchen and started cleaning up for the day with Brutus and Julius since the shop was closing in less than an hour. When the three of us finished up, we returned to the table where we were sitting earlier to observe Mama talking to the Stepford wives. A few minutes later, Romulus whispered something in her ear. She grew wide-eyed, before nodding her head as she went back to talking to Hestia and Themis while he approached our table.

"Hey boys, me and Cicero are gonna need the two of you on an errand we gotta run," he said.

Brutus and Julius looked at each other, before Julius looked back at Romulus and shakily inquired, "And what if we say no?"

"Then your father would be the one to hear about it. And I don't think that would be in the best interest of you two or anyone else in your family. Now get off your fat asses and do what we say!" Romulus angrily exclaimed.

Julius gulped a little bit before standing up to follow Romulus. Brutus looked at me, his face already broken out in sweats, before he clenched his teeth and hesitantly followed. Cicero, who was already standing at the door, held it open for the three of them before lighting up yet another cigar.

I felt butterflies explode in my stomach as the four of them got into Romulus's car and pulled off. My eyes grew into a scowl as I went back to watching Mama, Themis and Hestia sip their lattes, munch on their pastries and giggle to their heart's content. Members of an organized crime outfit had just dragged two innocent, teenaged boys into their shenanigans, right before their very own eyes. And they didn't care.

Hestia took another sip of her latte. "Calliope, come sit with us!"

I sat still for yet another moment, giving them a piercing stare. It was already clear to me that Hestia and Themis were both highly superficial and fake. As for Mama, I just felt disgusted with her. I had no interest in getting to know her new friends. But I also didn't want any more drama at home, so I obliged and joined them, despite my reluctance.

When I sat down at their table, Hestia reached her hand out to me and said, "It's a pleasure to meet you Calliope, I'm Hestia."

Themis followed suit and introduced herself as well, "My name is Themis. I am very happy to meet you as well!"

I returned both of their handshakes all while faking a smile. "It's very nice to meet the two of you as well."

Mama turned to me and smiled cheerfully. "Calliope, they both have daughters who are around your age. Seeing that you're new to the neighborhood, I think it would be a good idea for you to hang out with the two of them. Maybe sometime next week? After all, it would be great for you to make some new friends around here!"

"I'm an English teacher at the local high school, so when summer's over, you're going to be seeing me a lot more!" Hestia said exuberantly before taking another sip of her coffee. "Isn't that exciting?"

I just slowly nodded and feigned joy in my response, "Oh yeah, it's very exciting to make new friends! I'm looking forward to all of it."

They continued to talk until closing time while I just sat there, adding my thoughts on a sporadic basis. My stomach sank at the thought of meeting their daughters and possibly having Hestia as my English teacher swirled around in my mind. I knew right then and there that my experience in Griffin was going to be hell. And this was only the second week.

A Walk In The Park

Tight knots formed in my stomach as I sat on the couch, waiting for Julius and Brutus to return. The lights were off and my head turned to the doorway whenever I heard the slightest creak, thinking they had finally returned home. Not even a marathon of Thespis & Melpomene movies could ease my anxiety.

It was almost 11:00 P.M. and as Melpomene undressed Thespis and pushed him onto the bed, readying yet another sex scene between the two, I heard the door unlock. Julius and Brutus had both finally made it home.

My heart leapt out of my chest as I sat up quickly. "Oh my god, I'm so happy you two are finally home! I hope the two of you are okay!"

Brutus, while rubbing his gut with a tensed up face said, "I'd love to tell you all about it sis, but I've been holdin' in a ham-and-cheese panini for six hours and I really gotta go. Like *now*."

As Brutus made his way to the downstairs bathroom, Julius began to make his way up the stairs with melancholy eyes, looking as somber as ever.

I got off the couch and ran over to him. "Julius, will you tell me what happened?"

Julius looked back at me and sadly said, "I don't wanna talk about it, Calliope."

"I want to know about what those scumbags made you do! Mama didn't even care when she saw those two criminals take you away. And you know Dad isn't gonna help! You can at least tell me!"

"I don't want to tell anyone. Not right now."

"Julius, please!"

Julius gave me a disgruntled look before he angrily responded, "Just leave me alone, sis," and made his way up the stairs.

For a minute, I stood where I was, stunned into silence. I heard Julius walk into his room and slam his door shut before I slowly crept back over to the couch. The movie was now showing Melpomene in a nightclub with some friends, but I was too concerned about both of my brothers to even pay attention. A few minutes later, Brutus came out of the bathroom and sat down on the velvet brown recliner.

"You alright, sis?" he leaned over and asked me with a worried tone.

"No, I'm not. I was so worried for you and Julius and now Julius won't even tell me what went on," I answered with butterflies in my chest and a lump in my throat.

Brutus patted me on the knee reassuringly. "We're okay. And that's all that counts."

"But I want to know what happened. And why is Julius so upset?"

Brutus's eyes widened as he paused for a moment before saying, "In all honesty, I really don't know."

"You don't?" I asked in frustration.

"Yeah... matter of fact, I actually don't even really remember nothin'! That Megalopolis or whatever they call it is one weird place. Julius probably don't remember much either," Brutus answered with a shrug, "But hey, we made it out alive at least."

"Oh... okay," I replied reluctantly before laying down on the couch. Brutus picked up the remote and, without asking, changed the channel to reruns of *A Different World*. I honestly didn't even care. After worrying about the two of them all night, I needed some shut-eye and dozed off promptly afterward.

* * *

The red-tint of sunlight at the crack of dawn peered through the living room windows. Brutus opened his eyes slowly, wiped the drool off his cheek and covered his mouth as he let out a prolonged yawn. Smacking his lips, he turned to his right to see Calliope, still peacefully at rest on the couch. He turned to his left to look at the dark-gold, wooden clock hanging above the entertainment center. It was 5:45 A.M. Brutus stood up and stretched a little bit before making his way up to the upstairs bathroom that he and Julius shared.

He looked down the hallway, only to see that all of the doors were closed as he made his way to the bathroom. Not even a second after he opened the door, Brutus was met with the sound of Julius yelling at him.

"Whoa! You need to learn how to knock, man!" Julius exclaimed, his arms covered in soap suds as he reclined in the bathtub.

Brutus flinched, before he smirked. "Brother, you've been saying that since we were kids. If I didn't learn back then, then I ain't gonna learn now."

"Well, I'm not gonna let you have a BM while I'm takin' a bath, bro. There's three other bathrooms in this house for you to use," Julius bluntly expressed.

"I was actually about to take a shower, but since you're up, I'd like to talk to you," Brutus retorted.

"Talk to me about what? Last night? Ain't nothin' to talk about!" Julius explained, the slight shake in his voice indicating his nervousness.

"Oh yeah there is," Brutus further retorted as he closed the bathroom door and sat on the side of the tub, "Don't remember much, but I remember you was actin' real funny about somethin' on the way home."

Julius reclined his head on the back of the tub, closing his eyes and shaking his head as he stated, "I really don't wanna talk about it, and you know damn well you don't wanna hear it."

"Maybe I do," Brutus replied with a softened voice and a sincere, relaxed look in his eyes.

Julius slowly opened his eyes and looked at Brutus. He gathered himself for a moment before he asked, "Why do you care so much?"

Brutus briefly winced and raised his left eyebrow, puzzled as to why Julius would ask that, but he placed his hand on his chest as he answered, "Look, I know I may be a pain in the ass, but you're my brother. Why should I not care?"

Julius looked away towards the ceiling and exhaled, and then began, "That club Cicero and Romulus took us to last night?"

"Yeah?" Brutus asked in reply.

"There's this guy that works there, his name is Pothos. I met him at the pizza joint across the street from the bakery the day after we moved out this way."

"You mean the bouncer?"

"Yeah, that's who I'm talking about."

"Um, okay? So what about him?" Brutus asked.

Julius took a pause before he answered, "Well, I saw him and said 'what's up' and we started talking…"

"Uh, alright, and?" Brutus interrupted.

Julius looked back at Brutus and shook his head, before he explained, "We were in the middle of talking, and suddenly we both had to go to the bathroom."

Brutus's eyes widened and he even slightly tilted his head before asking, "Is that it?"

Julius took another pause, as if he were contemplating what to say next before he looked back at Brutus and nodded his head.

"So, let me get this straight? The reason why you was upset last night is because you were embarrassed about taking a dump at a nightclub?" Brutus asked, his frowned up face showing his disbelief.

Julius nodded again before saying, "Basically."

"Man, fuck outta here! There's something you're not telling me and I know it."

Julius smacked his lips and scowled his eyes before saying, "Yeah, there's a lot I ain't tellin' you! Cuz I know your loud-mouthed ass is gonna spill the beans to everybody!

Brutus let out a chuckle. "What kinda person do you take me for, bro?"

"Like when Perseus got expelled from school because you told everyone he sold weed to the basketball coach?" Julius noted.

Brutus just shrugged and said, "I mean, I was high as fuck that day."

"Man, that's always your damn excuse!" Julius scolded while shaking his head, "What about when you bragged to everybody about Medusa giving you a blowjob? Girl didn't show up to school for two whole weeks after that!"

"Alright, let me stop you right there, Julius! I wasn't bragging about it, I was going around warning people! That bitch had no idea how to suck a dick! Almost bit half my meat off and everything!"

"Oh yeah? What about when Saba almost got disowned, cuz he started dating that girl you wanted to get with and you went around telling people he was gay?"

"Whoa there, bro! That's all in the past! Who cares?" Brutus exclaimed while holding his hands up and laughing.

Julius looked away from him, scoffed and while rubbing his back with his soap covered hand mumbled, "I know I'd care if I got disowned."

"Hold up, where'd that come from?"

"Where did what come from?"

"Why are you all of sudden worried about getting disowned? You know you're pop's favorite!"

"The favorite is usually the one most likely to disappoint," Julius said with an air of uncertainty.

"Oh yeah? And how do you think you could disappoint dad?" Brutus asked with a raised eyebrow.

Julius looked up at Brtuus in disdain as he coolly said, "That's the same man who told me I deserved it that night, you know."

"Whoa, whoa, WHOA! What you bringin' THAT up for!?" Brutus cried out as he flailed around his hands.

"You still gonna try and act like it never happened, huh?" Julius asked as he shook his head.

Brutus then sighed as he bit back, "Oh yeah? Why should I? You ain't gonna forgive me either way."

Julius shot an angry glare at Brutus before he yelled, "You know what, bro? Just get outta here! You refuse to get it! Just leave me alone!"

Brutus just laughed as he stood up and left the bathroom, but not before looking back at his brother and obnoxiously whispering, "I don't know what it is, bro, but you actin' real suspect right now."

* * *

As much grief as I gave Griffin, I must say, Pompeii Square was a lovely space. Surrounded by oak trees, with a floor made up of light tan cobblestones, it felt like a modern day public square in Florence during the Renaissance. In one spot, there was an artist hard at work on a fresh canvas and next to them, one could observe a sweet, older woman weaving baskets by hand. Dancers, fortune tellers, guitar players, and various other sorts of buskers in between the kids goofing off and enjoying life. I made sure I had as much fun as possible, sitting on the bench and sipping my tea, just taking it all in, especially since I was not looking forward to meeting the daughters of Hestia and Themis.

I looked to my right and saw two girls approaching. It couldn't have been any more obvious, they both looked like miniature versions of their mothers. While her hair was blonde, Hestia's daughter, had a trying-too-hard look, akin to her mother's. She had on a navy blue, ruffled knee-length dress, with black lace stockings, black ballerina flats and a black beret trimmed with a lace net that covered a face of bold red lipstick and what had to have been a pound altogether of eyeliner, eye shadow and rouge.

Themis's daughter on the other hand, looked like she was on her way to a Tupperware party. With dirty blonde hair in a bouncy ponytail, she had on a bright pink dress, also blossoming out like a flower from her waist to her knees, with knee-high translucent white stockings and pink one-strap clogs adorning her feet.

Themis's daughter stared me up and down with a frowned-up

face as they walked towards me.

"You're Calliope, aren't you?" Hestia's daughter asked me, with a blunt tone in her voice.

I feigned a smile. "Why yes, I am."

"I'm Eris, Hestia's daughter."

"Moirai," the other said curtly, looking down at her pink polish painted fingernails.

"It's nice to meet the two of you," I said. I tried my hardest to sound cheerful, but every word out of my mouth sounded deadpan and monotone. Spending time with them seemed as exciting as listening to Brutus discuss his bathroom trips while I ate.

Eris and Moirai just looked at each other. With cold, bemused faces and moody eyes, I could see from a mile away they had no interest in hanging out with me.

"Well, let's get this done and over with," Eris said tactlessly as she sat down on the bench next to me. I just stared blankly at her, hoping she would instigate the conversation. Instead she continued to stare at me coldly.

Moirai, still standing, plainly asked, "Well, can you talk?"

I looked at her and bit my lip. "Yes, can you?"

Eris rolled her eyes, looked towards Moirai and motioned her to move closer. The two of them started whispering, making glances at me intermittently. I just sat there and took another sip of my tea while they were going on about whatever.

After they were done with their whisper session, Moirai turned to look at me. "Can you explain your sense of style? It's atrocious."

"Excuse me?" I replied, totally taken aback by her words. My eyes widened with simultaneous surprise and offense as my mouth dropped ajar.

"You're wearing acid washed overalls over a plain, white t-shirt with black all-star Converse shoes for starters," Eris quickly explained with a sarcastic smirk.

Moirai nodded. "And instead of having the decency to straighten that tangled mess of curls on your head this morning, you just wrapped a bandana around it. Have you no shame?"

"You look like a golliwog, 1990s style," Eris insulted with a straight face.

"Precisely. I don't know if you know this sweetie, but hip hop music video chic is not something that's appreciated in Griffin," Moirai added smugly with her arms crossed.

I smacked my lips and looked away from them to muster my comeback. "Well, I don't know if you know this, *sweetie*, but further up north in Atalan, a lot of people dress just like me and no one has a problem with it."

"Oh sure, if we're talking hoodlums in Inman and the Cascade, but my mother told me you're from Auburn, yes? I thought that neck of the woods was much more upscale than that," Eris sarcastically retorted.

"Ever heard of Neiman Marcus? Or Lord & Taylor?" Moirai asked, subtly rotating in place, showing off her gaudy 1950s style dress to me. "That's where the two of us go shopping. It's an upgrade from whatever flea market you pick up your rags from,"

"I'll remember that the next time I get 1992 confused with 1952," I said while smirking mischievously.

"Why I never!" Eris yelled with a scowled face. "I can't believe you have the audacity to insult actual fashion."

"Don't worry, I take it as a compliment," Moirai said, crossing her arms again and smugly eyeing me. "If this is the direction modern fashion is going in, then I'll stick to dressing like the girls from *Grease*. Thanks."

"You know what, forget you girls!" I exclaimed with furrowed eyebrows before picking up my cup of tea and storming away from them. Moirai and Eris were at first silent, but then they just looked at each other and burst out into a fit of laughter.

"Aww, don't run away! We were just telling you the truth about your horrible sense of fashion!" Eris yelled out while battling another incoming laugh. I didn't even care, I just walked away from them as I fast as I could.

"Calliope?" I heard a voice say.

I stopped, looked to my left, and saw Fortuna sitting in a small grass field, shaded by a drooping Spanish moss tree, smoking a cigarette while a guy sat next to her.

"Hi, Fortuna," I said perkily.

She motioned her hand towards me and exclaimed, "Come join us!"

I tilted my head under the moss and sat down as she introduced the guy next to her, "This is Pietas, my boyfriend. Pietas, Calliope."

"What up," he said to me with a slight drawl. He wore a bright red jersey, baggy jeans and white Nike Air Forces over his lanky build. Like Fortuna, his skin was olive, though slightly lighter in tone, with vacant, brown eyes and dark brown hair styled into an undercut.

"Nice to meet you," I replied.

"So, how did hanging out with Eriserable and Moirtem go?" Fortuna facetiously asked me with a smile.

"Huh?" I asked before laughing.

"I give everyone a nickname. Eris has this high and mighty attitude that makes people miserable, hence Eriserable. Moirai's face is so blank and motionless, it looks like she's posing for a post-mortem photograph. So I call her Moirtem."

"I didn't even spend ten minutes with them and I already completely understand where you're coming from," I said, laughing even louder.

"What were you doing hanging out with them anyway?" Fortuna asked while offering me a cigarette.

I took the cigarette and answered, "My mom became friends with their mothers and they set up a little playdate for us."

"Well I have no idea what Hestia the Hessian and Miss Cleaver were thinking," Fortuna replied stoically, "No offense but you represent just about everything those two girls hate."

"None taken," I said between puffs of smoke, making mental notes of the off color nicknames Fortuna had for every insufferable person I had met in Griffin.

"Well, you have some early preparation for your first day of school here. Trust me, Eris and Moriai are only two of fifty kids that make Pegasus High a living hell."

"At least I know what to expect," I said with a shrug as Fortuna let out a slight chuckle. Pietas remained silent, staring intently at the moss hanging above as me and Fortuna continued to chatter away. After a few minutes, Pietas went about his way as Fortuna and I left Pompeii Square and took a walk along Ponos Street.

"Why don't you come back to my place, Calliope? We can sneak one of my mom's bottles of scotch and smoke a bowl."

"Um, thanks for the invite, but I think I'm good," I declined with a laugh.

"Aww, come on!" Fortuna teased as we neared the pizza shop. We were still laughing when suddenly, Cicero barged out the door, shooting Fortuna an angry glare.

"Where the fuck have you been, huh?!" Cicero shouted at her.

Fortuna scowled at him as she bit back, "Oh, is that how it is? I'm not allowed to spend the night at my boyfriend's house!?"

I just looked on and gulped as Cicero scolded, "For three nights in a row!? And you didn't even bother to give me a call!? I was about to go down to the police station to file a missing person's report and everything! What the hell were you thinking!?"

Fortuna looked him up and down. "Like you wouldn't have told me no if I told you where I was going!"

Cicero's eyes widened before he shook his head and, in a softer voice, explained, "Uh-uh. My wife would have said no, but I would have said it's alright if you just told me. That's all you had to do."

"You only would have said it's okay after telling me how ungrateful I am," Fortuna retorted.

Cicero silently glared at her for a moment before closing his eyes. "Why do you think that all I want to do is argue with you?"

I scratched my neck and looked away as I muttered, "It's not like you have the most agreeable persona."

"Who the hell asked for your goddamn opinion!?" Cicero shouted at me, before he looked back to Fortuna and ordered, "I think we're gonna have to do this in the office, Fortuna. Talking to you is already hard enough without another brat in the vicinity."

"Ugh, fine," Fortuna bemoaned, before she looked back at me to somberly say, "Looks like I'm about to be grounded for the next couple of weeks. Guess I'll see you later, Calliope."

"Alright, Fortuna. Thanks for hanging out with me," I replied.

Fortuna smirked at me before she walked in, as Cicero looked at me in disdain before he said to her, "I don't think I approve of your new friend over here. Girl strikes me as nothing but trouble."

"Man, whatever!" I called out as he walked back into the pizza shop. Worried about Fortuna, I just stared at the pizza shop for a moment, before I closed my eyes and sighed when I heard the loud roar of a motorcycle coming down Ponos Street. I turned around and saw a Norton Commando pulling up behind me. The rider, wearing a red and black biker jacket and helmet, began to take his gloves off, only to take his jacket off to reveal the Tommy Hilfiger shirt underneath. Finally he took his helmet off.

I couldn't help but to pause and stare. He was the most handsome specimen I had ever seen in my life, with narrow eyes and smooth skin of a golden brown shade, both of which gleamed beneath the sunlight, a goatee adorned his long angular face as he took out a hair pick to fluff out his hi-top fade.

As I silently looked on at him in admiration, from his fresh Timberlands and baggy jeans to the twinkling gold, hoop earrings in his ears, he turned his head to look at me. My eyes bulged out of my head as I let out a nervous smile and tried to maintain my composure. He looked at me in wide-eyed confusion at first, before his face relaxed into a smirk.

"Everything cool with you?" He asked in a smooth, smoky voice with a New York-ish drawl.

"Oh, um, I'm fine!" I stammered, "Just admiring that... nice bike of yours!"

"I see," he said with a laugh, "Well, how about a little introduction. My name's Troy. What's yours?"

"Calliope," I said breathily, "I get the vibe you're not from around these parts. What brings you out this way?"

"Is that how it is? I could say the same about you! Wasn't expecting to see no black girl walkin' down the street in Griffin," Troy laughed. "You are right though - I'm not from around these parts. I live over in The Cascade, matter of fact. But I do got a cousin around here."

"Do you really?" I asked.

"Yup, sure do, but I haven't seen her since we were little," he answered.

"Aww, how come?" I asked

Troy just shrugged before explaining, "According to my uncle Cleon, her dad and his family don't want us anywhere near her. Sounds like a real messy situation, so I'm not all that eager to get back in touch with her to be honest with you."

"Your uncle... Cleon?" I asked.

Troy took pause as he stared at me for a moment before he said, "Yeah. Do you know him?"

"The name sounds a bit familiar to me, but I can't put my finger on where I heard it from," I shrugged, despite the fact I knew that I had read it from one of the notes in the box a few weeks prior.

"I see," Troy replied with a raised eyebrow, "Anyway, to answer your question, I was actually looking for a new job. Wanted to branch out from the family business and try something different. And I see that I'm in luck; looks like this pizza joint over here is hiring."

I took a look behind me only to see a "Help Wanted" sign in the window of the pizza shop. I saw Troy hop off of his bike and proceed to walk in, before I swooped in to block the doorway with a nervous smile on my face.

Troy scratched his neck as he looked at me and asked, "What's the big idea here?"

"Just looking out for you. The guy who owns this place is a pretty big jerk, so you really don't want to work here," I explained.

Troy just looked at me for a moment before he closed eyes and chuckled, "Alright, thanks for the heads up then I guess. Know of any other shops on this street looking for help?"

I looked across the street at The Cornucopia and sighed, before I went on to suggest, "You could try the bakery and café across the street. They might be looking for someone."

"Oh a café, huh? Just like my family's business!" Troy noted, "Well, I guess it never hurts to apply. Thanks for letting me know."

"You're welcome. Good luck," I said. Troy looked back at me with a curt head nod as he made his way across the street. Once he walked inside The Cornucopia, I just sighed before I plodded back home.

Secrets

As I walked into our home, I breathed a sigh of relief. I knew everyone would be away from home and I needed silence. I just wanted to be alone. I made my way up the stairs to my room. As usual every door was closed, but I could tell I was not alone. I heard laughter from Julius's room, which I was happy to hear. It was hard to see him so unhappy after having to leave Bolina. I couldn't help but giggle when the laughter transitioned into moaning and the creaking of the bed springs. Maybe Julius had found himself another girl.

I took to writing once more to get my mind off the disastrous life I had already been experiencing in the suburbs of Atalan. Having gotten myself lost in my own sea of words again, I heard the door to Julius's room open around twenty minutes later. With a mischievous smile, I hopped out of bed to crack my door open and get a look at his new girlfriend. To my surprise, my eyes were greeted to the sight of Julius talking and laughing with a large, bald-headed man with sepia-toned skin.

I quietly re-closed the door and placed my back against it to ponder what I had just seen. I could have sworn what I heard was a lovemaking session. The moaning? The bed creaking? If I was sure of what I'd heard, why was a man walking out of his room?

I walked over to my bed and started writing again. After twenty minutes, I felt a rumble in my stomach. I had gotten so upset over what happened in Pompeii Square earlier, I forgot to get something to eat. I assumed that Julius and his mystery friend had already left, so I made my way to the kitchen, but it turned out I was wrong. I was welcomed to the sight of Julius sitting on a stool next to the kitchen island as his friend was standing over the stove, cooking.

I stepped back and hid around the corner for a moment, carefully observing what was going on. Julius's eyes were hanging low as he glanced seductively at the man standing at the stove with a sly grin on his face. After a couple minutes, I saw the man walk from the stove over to Julius and look at him longingly before he wrapped his large, chiseled arms around his neck and gave him a deep, passionate kiss.

Immediately taken aback by the sight, I hopped from behind the wall. "JULIUS????"

They both stopped mid-kiss and with large, frightened eyes turned to look at me. I saw the man back away from Julius while remaining fixated on me as Julius quietly whispered, "Aww shit," while putting his hand over his face.

I walked towards Julius and placed my hand on his shoulder before I assured, "Do you want to talk about this, bro? I promise not to tell anyone else if you don't want me to."

"I guess I have no choice right now, do I?" Julius muttered with a slightly shaky tone in his voice as he got off the barstool and we walked over to the living room.

"So, Julius, what's going on?" I asked.

"Calliope, I'm bisexual," Julius told me, somewhat somberly.

While twirling my hair in my fingers as I mustered my response, I then asked, "But, you've always liked girls, is this something new?"

"Yeah, and boys too. I've realized it ever since I was a kid, but I was too afraid to ever tell anyone, let alone act out on it."

"Julius, you know I would never judge you."

"I know you wouldn't, Cali. And neither would Isis or Atum, but I can't say the same for everyone else. You and I both know Dad would disown me on the spot and Mama would probably just try and pray it away or something. As for Brutus, well, we'd never hear the end of it."

"Well, maybe just give it some time. You are eighteen after all. If you wait to come out to the family after you've already been living on your own for a while, what's the worst that could happen?" I suggested.

Julius, who was fixated on the floor briefly scoffed before he replied, "Cali, you really don't know that much about how Atalan works. Dad is still the patriarch of our House, and he still has power over me until I'm thirty. It doesn't matter if I live on my own and took my piece before I told him, he could still have my life ruined."

I slightly leaned back in shock after he said that. Every time I thought I had a pretty good comprehension of the rules and flow of society in Atalan, I would hear something else that threw all that knowledge out of the window.

"So, you're telling me we're our dad's property until we reach thirty?" I asked with a slight stutter.

"Basically," Julius answered matter-of-factly.

"Well, Julius, I don't want you to feel you have to live your life in hiding. I want you to be happy."

"Well, for now, that's what I'm gonna have to do. It's the only thing that's safe. I'm happy with Pothos either way."

"Is that his name, Pothos?" I asked warmly.

"Yes, it is," Julius answered with a chuckle.

"How'd you guys meet?"

"At Cicero's pizza shop, believe it or not. It was a couple of days before The Cornucopia opened. I went in to grab a slice, saw him at the counter and we just made casual conversation. Over time it was just like, he'd stop by just to say hi, and we came to realize we had a thing for each other."

"Well, I'm glad you've found someone else to love, bro," I said with a warm smile.

"So am I, Cali. So am I," Julius replied while nodding his head. We heard someone knock on the wall. Both of us looked up only to see it was Pothos, walking out of the kitchen with spatula in hand. He gave me an awkward glance, which I returned with a smile. He relaxed his shoulders and let out a sigh of relief afterward.

"Lunch anyone?" Pothos asked us.

Julius looked at me. "You wanna join, Calliope?"

I smiled and said, "Yeah, I'll join you guys."

The three of us sat at the kitchen table and dug into Pothos's chicken parmesan over penne and tomato sauce. I made myself a plate and joined in on the conversation.

"So, you must be Calliope, right?" Pothos asked.

"That would be me," I answered, "It's very nice to meet you, Pothos."

"Hey Cali, how did things go with those two girls earlier?" Julius asked.

I rolled my eyes and scoffed, "It was a complete disaster. They had to have been the most stuck-up girls I have ever met."

Julius and Pothos both laughed as Pothos advised, "You're gonna have to get used to that. Just about all of the kids around here are spoiled and snobby little brats."

"Yeah, I figured," I said with a laugh. Although slightly uncomfortable at first, as the three of us talked, it quickly became less and less relevant to me that I was in the presence of a same-sex couple. Pothos had a bright and bubbly aura to him; a very friendly and outgoing person with a great sense of humor in spite of the intimidating exterior he belied. Julius was still Julius, kind and wise as always.

In the middle of our conversation, Dad walked into the kitchen. It was the first time I had seen him in days. Dapper as usual, he looked towards us with a slight frown on his face as his attention seemed primarily focused on Pothos and Julius.

He walked a little bit closer to the table and looked directly at Julius. "Who is this guy why are you two sitting so close together?" he asked in an accusatory tone. I couldn't help but gulp when I heard him say that. His tone said everything about what he was thinking.

Julius managed to keep his cool with a calm smirk on his face. "Dad, this is my friend Pothos. I invited him over for a swim in the pool earlier. When we were done, we came in the house and he offered to cook. That's all."

Dad let out a slight, but still jarring, smack of his lips before replying, "Well, next time the two of you sit down at my table, keep a few more inches between yourselves. You two look far too comfortable with each other right now." I could tell by the way he said that that he didn't exactly believe him.

As he started to walk away, I snappily questioned, "Well, what have *YOU* been doing?"

Dad turned around and looked towards me with furrowed eyebrows and a snarled grimace on his face. "That's none of your business Calliope, and don't you dare talk to me like that ever again." Afterwards he stormed away from the kitchen and up the stairs.

"Calliope?" Julius frantically asked me.

"Yes?" I coolly answered in reply.

"What were you thinking?"

"Exactly what I asked. What the hell has he been doing? I'm getting sick and tired of his elusive nonsense."

Julius looked down and sighed. "If I were you, I wouldn't ask. Ever."

"Well maybe I'm just tired of the secrecy in this house," I said as I finished my food, "It was nice spending time with the two of you, but I'm going to have to excuse myself to my room."

Julius just nodded as I made my way out of the kitchen and up the stairs. Upon entering my room, I immediately focused upon the box. I walked over to the dresser, picked up the box, sat on the bed and started rummaging through its contents. There was one folded, red piece of paper in the corner that caught my eye in particular. I paused to stare at it for a moment. My stomach oddly started to sink, as if I were expecting to read something even darker than allegories of pyromania or mind control upon unfolding it. Of course, my curiosity got the best of me and I picked up that piece of paper and started reading it.

"September 15th, 1977

Today marks six months since March 15th; the day my angel was born. As I look into her deep, dark brown eyes, complemented by a constantly giggling face and a beautiful mane of coiled black hair, I'm reminded of how she's literally the only thing that makes my fears, worries and anxieties go away.

For the past two months, she only smiles, babbles and laughs whenever we move from place to place. She doesn't even cry anymore. It's a true miracle indeed that she is able to remain happy in the face of all of this adversity.

Thankfully, I've recently been able to track down The Oracle. She let me move in with her at her villa in Savannah Beach, but she is a creature of nomadic nature. When she moves, then my angel and I will have no choice but to do the same.

I really have no idea where to go anymore. Odysseus has called for open season on our kind. Nowhere in Atalan is safe for any of us. My love, Homer, has been rotting away in the dungeons of The Acropolis for nearly a year. He couldn't even witness the birth of our daughter. I cry every night just thinking about it.

Every sanctuary for the Mystics has been exposed. The diner building in the Cascade? Ransacked. The halfway house in the Five Points? Not only was it defaced with anti-Mystic graffiti, but even Atalan's darling council-bitch, Narcissus, publicly pointed the finger at them, alleging they housed "crones," so we had no choice but to retreat.

I've talked to The Oracle day and night about this ever since moving in with her. However powerful she may be though, I understand that she can only do so much to ward off outside forces, especially being a woman of such high social standing.

I feel so lost and alone. My friends and peers have all agreed to talk to each other as little as possible as another means of avoiding exposure, and yet, without them around, I feel even more vulnerable.

I really just don't know what to do anymore. My angel is the only thing that keeps me going."

"Well, that was intense," I thought to myself as I re-folded the piece of paper and put it back in the box. The anecdote managed to create more questions than it answered. What exactly did she mean by "our kind" or "mystics"? And why was Odysseus calling for their "kind" to be hunted back in 1977? Also, who was this "Oracle?"

As I closed the box and placed it back on the dresser, my stomach sank once more as another detail occurred to me. In the note, she said that March 15th, 1977 was the day her baby was born. My date of birth happened to be the exact same day.

This House Is Not A Home

I laid in my bed, staring at the ceiling for hours while my mind raced with mental re-reads of the note. I just couldn't shake the coincidence of her daughter's birthday. I suddenly heard a knock at the door. "Who is it?"

"It's your little brother. I brought food for you," Atum said from the other side of the door.

I got out of my bed and opened the door to see Atum, with a plate of food and a glass of lemonade in his hands. He extended them out towards me, but stared with heavy eyes and a disconcerted facial expression.

"Well, thanks for bringing up dinner for me, but what's the matter little bro?" I asked him.

He walked into my room, put the plate and glass on the dresser and said, "I'm worried about you, Cali. You've been keeping to yourself too much and I don't like it. Why didn't you come down to dinner?"

I smirked, patted him on the shoulder and assured, "I've just had a lot on my mind lately, but I'll be okay! No need to worry about me.

"Is that it? You know can talk to me sis," Atum said while creasing his eyebrows and folding his arms.

"Yeah, I'm pretty sure," I answered with slight hesitation,

given that there was a lot I wasn't telling him. I wish I could have spilled the beans to Atum, but he really wasn't the right person for it. Times like these made me miss Herc even more.

Atum's eyes shifted away from me and towards the dresser with his finger pointed towards the box. "What's that?"

"What's what?" I asked as a lump formed in my throat and I tried to pretend I didn't know what he was talking about.

"That box on your dresser. I've never seen it before."

"Oh, *that*! I've had that dusty old thing ever since I was a kid! I put it up a long time ago, and when I unpacked my boxes here, I decided to go ahead and make use of it again!" I fibbed enthusiastically.

Atum relaxed his face. "I see. Well, if you need anything, I'll be in my room." He walked out of my room and shut the door behind him. I put one of my favorite CD's in the boombox, Michael Jackson's *Dangerous* and started to eat as "Jam" blared out the speakers. Strangely enough, I felt an odd sense of relief as I listened to the music. If only it was always as simple as turning on some music.

* * *

Under the starry sky on a midsummer's night, Herc sat under the gazebo in the Garden of Artemis with his face in hands, reflecting on another long day working for the Peloponnesians.

They don't pay me enough to put up with their shit, Herc thought to himself as he heard the gate of the garden to their mansion open with a loud creak behind him. He turned around only to see Zeu-se and Calliope's dad, Pan, walk out while having a conversation as the gate slammed shut behind them. He quickly looked away, to help ensure they wouldn't notice him as he kept his ears open.

What are those two shady bastards up to now? Herc wondered. He looked over his shoulder to see Pan with a lit cigar, talking with Zeu-se who had a sly smirk on his face, nodding in silence.

"See, I tricked Demeter into working with the Griffin Mafia on her new café out that way," he overheard from Pan.

"Ah," Zeu-se replied before he added, "Is the girl working there?"

"Yes," Pan answered.

"Well, whatever you do, don't let anyone know of her background," Zeu-se cryptically responded.

"Of course not! She must stay in her place before she's sent to Teleiotita once she turns eighteen." He took another hit of cigar. "I can't take any chances. My good-for-nothing was friends with many south siders... they could have been spying on us the whole time."

Zeu-se chuckled. "I don't think you have anything to worry about, my friend. My wife has manipulated quite a few minds over the years... a necessary precaution given what we did."

"Good looking out, Zeu-se," Pan said, nodding before his face curled up in a grimace. "But what about Cleon?"

Zeu-se just burst out laughing and scoffed. "Last I heard, that fat Puerto Rican had his soul taken from him, so we don't have anything to worry about!"

"Well, I can rest a little easier at night after hearing that news," Pan laughed as Zeu-se joined.

Herc turned back away. "What the hell are they talking about?"

He looked over his shoulder once more to see the two of them finishing up their conversation. Pan put out his cigar and the two of them re-entered Zeu-se's mansion through the gate.

Herc stood up from the gazebo and lit a cigarette before he saw someone peering out of the same window that caught Calliope's attention a month earlier. Herc chuckled as he flashed a peace sign to the figure and made his way home.

* * *

Brutus and I were busy readying The Cornucopia for the morning rush. He turned on the coffee machines and I baked the bagels, muffins and other breakfast foods, but there wasn't so much as a word between us. Aside from him waking me up, we had been totally silent that entire morning. I was almost waiting for him to say something rude and obnoxious just to break the deafening effect of the quiet.

"So did Julius tell you he's a faggot now?" he asked with a straight face.

I was taken aback by his tone. "Yes, I know he's in a relationship with a man. How did you know?"

"I walked in on him fudge packin' that dude the other night."

"Oh," I quickly replied, trying to ignore how crude he was being.

"Crazy, huh? I mean, I love my bro no matter what, but that's just nasty right there," Brutus said, expressing his disdain in the most nonchalant way possible.

"I was weirded out at first too, but I met Pothos last week. I may not be used to his lifestyle, but he seemed like a nice enough guy. Besides, Julius is still the same person, so I'm not gonna try to get in the way of his happiness," I politely retorted.

"Well, that's what makes *him* happy," Brutus said snidely. "I ain't the type to support the kind of relationship where a dude is letting another give it to him up the booty."

"Ugh, Brutus, you're impossible! And gross!" I exclaimed, looking away from him and going back to organizing the counter display.

I looked at the clock and saw it was five minutes after opening time. I bolted over to the door to unlock it. As I approached the translucent, glass door, I noticed two figures standing behind it, but I was more focused on the lock than I was on them.

"Good morning and welcome to The Cornucopia," I said as I opened the door with a wide smile on my face, which quickly faded away when I looked up and saw the two people were Hestia and Themis, who returned my greeting with blank stares.

"Well, if it isn't the antisocial butterfly," Hestia said sarcastically.

Themis promptly added, "Our daughters told us all about your little verbal scuffle with them in the square last week. How rude of you."

I clenched my teeth and responded, "Ma'am, I don't think either one of them wanted to be friends with me in the first place. They didn't even give me a chance before they went straight to insulting how I dress."

"Perhaps you could learn a lesson or two from them in that department," Hestia interrupted as she coolly looked up and down at my outfit, which consisted of ripped jeans, Nike sneakers and a black wife-beater style tank top.

They walked in and Brutus made his way to the register. "Is Demeter here today?" Themis asked curtly before he could get a word out.

"Not right now, she'll be here by 9:00," Brutus answered politely. Hestia and Themis both looked at each other, with Hestia rolling her eyes before they both proceeded to order.

Their true colors are finally showing, I thought to myself as I made my way back into the kitchen. Brutus made their coffees, and I heated up their bagels. When it came time to serve them, I nonchalantly walked to their table, before forcefully putting down their coffee mugs and throwing both of their plates on the table.

I then smiled and snidely said to them, "You two lovely ladies enjoy your breakfast." I walked away while they stared at me with their eyes askew and their mouths agape in awe.

"The nerve of that rude, ungrateful brat," I heard Hestia complain. Not like I cared.

"Calliope, I didn't think you had all of that sass in you girl!" Brutus chuckled and motioned out for me to pound his fist.

I smiled and gave him thanks, but didn't return the fist-bump. "Be more open-minded and accepting with our brother first, then I'll give you as many fist-bumps as you'd like."

That morning was a relatively slow one, with only two more customers entering the cafe before Mama showed up. Without so much as a good morning to me or Brutus, she walked right over to her new friends with a bright, cheery smile on her face. But as she talked to Hestia and Themis, it quickly turned into a frown. With Hestia and Themis both periodically eyeing me for the duration of their entire conversation, I could tell they were telling mom about everything that transpired earlier this morning. I just smirked and shook my head as I tidied things up around the kitchen and seating area.

"CALLIOPE!?" she shouted.

I paused in the middle of wiping a table down, only to look at her and sassily asked in reply, "Yes mama?"

She grabbed my arm and dragged me to the office at the back of the store. After entering the office, she shut the door, and looked at me with softly scowled eyes and a subtle frown for a few seconds, before she began yelling.

"I can't believe you, Calliope! What's the matter with you!?"

"What's the matter with what? Hestia and Themis aren't nice people," I retorted nonchalantly. "And neither are their daughters."

"So you would rather be friends with a south-sider? Or working-men like Leto's son? As a Noble, you need to build connections and relationships with people like them! People of *your* social standing! That's the way it is in Atalan, always has been!" Demeter explained with a tone of condescension.

"At least Herc accepted me for me! I'm not going to be something I'm not to get in the good graces of someone who's never going to accept me anyway!" I snapped back.

Mom looked like she was readying herself to yell again, but instead she closed her eyes and quickly inhaled and exhaled before she firmly, but calmly said, "You just don't understand how it works. You do not associate with those of a standing beneath yours, for that may as well make you one of them. Our house is one of Upper Noble standing, Calliope; fast on our way to becoming Royals. But with the route you're going on here in Griffin, I fear that you may cross the line with the wrong person. The very person that could render you an Untouchable."

I just stared at her. In Atalan society, Untouchables were the lowest of the low. The banished. The pariahs of the pariahs. The rats of Atalan. A punishment worse than being thrown in the dungeons of The Acropolis. Worse than even death.

After a brief pause, I scowled at her. "I can't believe you!"

I ran out of her office and onto Ponos Street, where I wouldn't know anyone. The Cornucopia was filled with bad vibes. My family's house was filled with bad vibes. And I definitely didn't want to go to Pompeii Square, lest I run into Eris and Moirai again. I may as well have been chasing pavement, which I did until I got to the steps of The Griffin Polis Council House.

As I ran past the fanciful, Parthenon-inspired building, I accidentally stepped on a man's black oxford shoes. After a few steps, I came to a halt, turned around and saw that I had scuffed one of his shoes. I could see in his cold face that he wasn't amused. A tall, lanky man in a dark brown suit, he had salt-and-pepper hair styled into an Ivy League style haircut with a side part, steely blue-grey eyes, pale, niveous skin, a long nose and tightly pressed lips. I couldn't help but gulp as I looked him in the eye.

"I'm so sorry, sir! I didn't notice you standing there," I apologized with a slight shakiness.

He nodded, barely breaking façade. "Next time, you better watch where you're going. It's not nice to scuff a man's shoes, especially not those of the Magister of this polis!" My stomach sank to the ground upon hearing he was the Magister of Griffin.

"I apologize, sir. I've had a really rough day," I said hesitantly.

"Young woman, you are to address me by my official title: Magister Hadrian," he told me with a callous tone, not even so much as shirking in his frigid, aloof demeanor.

I felt my body tighten up. "I won't let it happen again."

"You'd best keep your word. I am no fan of tomfoolery," he said callously.

Magister Hadrian turned away from me and began to walk in the opposite direction. I decided to walk to Pompeii Square after all, breathing a sigh of relief after seeing no sign of Moirai or Eris. Instead, I saw Fortuna sitting on one of the benches. Smoking another cigarette, she smiled and waved for me to join her.

"Hey Fortuna," I greeted, sitting next to her. "I thought you were grounded?"

"So did I. But he let me off the hook and said 'don't let it happen again,'" Fortuna laughed, mocking Cicero's accent.

"I see," I laughed. "How are you today?"

She took another hit of her cigarette and sighed. "Can't really complain. Me and my dad got into another argument earlier, but I'm used to that at this point."

"How surprising," I said sarcastically.

"I don't want to hate him, but he's such an asshole! It's like he doesn't know how to love me or something. I try to talk to him and spend time together, only for us to get into it. Then he just gives me some money and tells me to buy another CD of 'the weird music I listen to,' so I'll shut up."

"That's how I'm beginning to feel. Mama seems to only care about being the black Martha Stewart and Dad's never home. By the way, do you have any idea what he's been doing with the Mafia?"

Fortuna shrugged. "I'm not the right person to ask. I try not to pay attention to them. It works for the most part, because most of my family likes to pretend I don't exist for some reason."

"Is that so?"

Fortuna laughed. "It sure is. Not that I'm complaining. Sometimes, I wonder if I was adopted. I mean, you've only met Cicero and Romulus, but have you noticed that I don't look like either one of them?"

I paused to think. "Yeah, you're right now that I think about it."

"I don't look like anyone on either side of my family. Everyone on my dad's side has brown or dark blonde hair and green, hazel or blue eyes. As for my mom and her family, they're all blonde and pale. And then you have me: dark brown eyes and black hair. I guess I have the olive skin as my dad's family, but it's darker than everyone else's. It's kinda weird when I think about it. And I used to get a lot of shit for it from them as a child, but I take it as a good thing now," Fortuna explained with a laugh as I joined in. Shortly afterward, two girls approached us. One was short with glasses, curly, blonde hair and an average build, and the other was tall and slender with her brown hair tied up in a scrunchie.

"Well, well, well, if it isn't *UnFortuna* the Loner!" teased the girl with blonde hair.

"She doesn't appear to be a loner anymore, Lethaea," the other girl laughed facetiously. "Looks like she's friends with our new token minority! Don't you just love integration?"

"Hey, don't talk about my friend like that, Sidero!" Fortuna defended, rolling her eyes. "Why are you guys messing with us, anyway? Why don't you go hop on the yachts your parents have in Savannah Beach and let us normal people enjoy our time away from the shitshow you've all created at Pegasus."

Lethaea and Sidero just looked at each other and laughed. "So you accuse us of being racist, only to assume we have yachts?! How hypocritical!" Sidero retorted.

"I'm still stuck on the part where you called yourself normal," Lethaea noted before a fit of laughter.

"Oh no! I stereotyped some poor little rich white girls!" Fortuna mocked. "Here's an idea: let me and my friend continue to mind our own business like we were doing, while you two hop and skip on over to Medea's house."

They both snickered while Fortuna and I looked at each other and rolled our eyes before Lethaea spoke. "Will do, *UnFortuna*! Come on, Sidero! We should go about our way as this picture of racial harmony unfolds. The new black girl in town is friends with the girl whose ethnicity we can never seem to figure out - isn't it wonderful!?"

Fortuna smacked her lip and threw her hands up. "I'm getting sick and tired of people asking *what* I am! I'm Italian! Get it through your heads!"

Lethaea and Sidero began to walk away, only for Sidero to turn around snidely. "Are you sure you aren't saying that so no one will ask for your green card? Because you have got to be the most Mexican-looking Italian I have ever seen."

They walked off as Fortuna shook her head and groaned. "Ugh! Why is everyone around here so stupid and annoying?!"

"I can see that. Out of everyone I've met, you're the only person that I like."

Fortuna nodded. "I feel really bad for you, moving out this way. You are NOT gonna like Pegasus High. Not one bit."

"I'm dreading it already."

* * *

Demeter and Brutus were cleaning up The Cornucopia after yet another successful day. After Brutus washed all the dishes, Demeter swept and mopped the floor and wiped all the tables down. They turned the lights off and locked the door as they walked out. As Brutus approached the car, Demeter was eyeing the pizza shop across the street.

"Brutus?" Demeter asked as Brutus stood next to the car, waiting for her to open the door.

"Yeah Mama?" Brutus asked irritably.

"I'm feeling a little bit hungry and I'm not in the mood to cook. Do you want some pizza?"

"I'm cool, moms. I just wanna go home, drink and smoke up

to be real with you," he answered.

Demeter rolled her eyes and sighed. "As you always do. Well, I'm going to grab a pizza."

"Aw, is that how it is? You gonna make me walk home?" Brutus whined.

Demeter began to cross the street, before looking back at him. "That's not what I said. You can wait right here until the pizza's ready."

"Whatever! It's only a ten minute walk." Brutus began to walk down Ponos Street towards their house as Demeter rolled her eyes and made her way into the pizza shop. She ordered a supreme pizza and a pepperoni pizza, before sitting at one of the red-and-white cloth covered tables as she waited for her order. Cicero emerged out of the office in the back, yelling into his cell phone.

"What do ya mean you need the money for Mr. Phil!? That man rakes in thousands of dollars a weekend from that nightclub anyway!" he yelled as Demeter turned to observe. "Okay Remus, fine! I'll loan you guys the money! And you better pay it back this time!" He hung up and slammed his phone on one of the tables. He sat down and began to mumble to himself as Demeter continued to watch.

"Are you okay, Cicero?" Demeter asked with worry.

Cicero looked at her. "Hell no, I'm not okay! All I'm trying to do is run my pizza joint in peace, only to get the goddamn short end of the stick again!"

Demeter looked away before she smirked and walked over to sit at his table. "Do you wanna talk about it?"

Cicero rubbed his hands and looked at her. "My family thinks I'm the one that needs to do all the dirty work, since I'm the baby brother."

"You mean to tell me you're the *baby* of the family?" Demeter interrupted in disbelief.

Cicero laughed. "That's right. I got two brothers and two sisters, all older, shorter and smaller than me. Don't ask me how that happened."

"I mean, you do run a pizza shop," Demeter joked.

"Oh yeah? You just pushed a button lady!" Cicero defended in jest. "But yeah, always been a big boy. I finally slimmed down in my twenties, but then something really... weird happened in my thirties and I just let myself go again."

"Something weird ? How so?"

Cicero blew his lips and shrugged. "I don't even know. It was like I was myself one day, and the next, everything about me felt different. Now, everyone's scared of me... because I'm afraid of myself."

"You're... afraid of yourself?"

"Your pizzas are ready!" the cook called out.

"Thank you, I'll pick them up in a moment."

She turned back to Cicero. "Yeah, I'm terrified of myself. I feel like there's all this rage and anger, struggling to break out, ya know? It's why I have such a strained relationship with my daughter. I'd kill myself if I ever did anything to harm her. These feelings are just so uncontrollable, I try to keep my distance from her."

Demeter looked down and touched his hand. "I think I can relate. I have an issue of my own that's hard to control sometimes. I should go to therapy to get it under control, but my husband insists that church, and church alone, will solve everything."

"I don't even think that would help me. Therapy, anger management, hell, even yoga. I've tried it all. Not a single thing works." Cicero looked away and closed his eyes with a sigh. "Much as I miss him, gotta say, it's times like these I'm happy the other kid ain't around."

"So Fortuna isn't your only child?" Demeter asked with a raised eyebrow as Romulus walked in the door. Demeter quickly pulled away from Cicero and gasped when she saw him approaching their table.

"Hey, Demeter," Romulus inquired as he placed his hand on her shoulder. "How's everything at The Cornucopia going?"

"Everything's going great, Romulus! Thank you so much for all of your help," Demeter answered with a nervous smile.

"Happy to hear it," Romulus replied before looking at Cicero. "We need to talk, little brother."

"Remus already told me everything!" Cicero protested with a scowl.

Romulus shook his head. "Forty-one years old and you still haven't put that damn attitude in check. Do you wanna do this in your office or upstairs?"

Cicero's eyes grew wide as he gulped. "I don't go upstairs in this building. *Ever.* You know that."

"Well, come on then! Let's have a talk, brother to brother," Romulus demanded as Cicero shook his head and followed him into the office.

"Hey, Cicero?" Demeter called out as both brothers paused to look at her. "After you're done, do you want to meet me at The Cornucopia, so we can continue to talk over a cup of coffee?"

Cicero smirked and nodded. "I think I'd like that."

He walked into the office, as did Romulus, but not before pausing to look at Demeter with disdain. Then, he chuckled and smirked ominously before walking into the office and closing the door. Demeter picked up her pizzas, placed them in her car and opened the door to The Cornucopia. She made two cups of coffee, placed both of them on the table and eagerly awaited Cicero's arrival.

* * *

"*GET UP OFF MY BACK! SAVE A HEART ATTACK! AIN'T NOBODY HUMPIN' AROUND!*" Brutus sang loudly to Bobby Brown's newest song, "Humpin' Around," while while laying down on the couch, as three empty beer bottles and a slowly waning bottle of bourbon sat on the coffee table. As the sounds of new jack swing and g-funk pounded from the stereo in the living room, he fired up a blunt. Crossed in the realms of two different levels of intoxication, he gave up trying to sing along to song lyrics and burst out in a fit of sleepy laughter. A few minutes later, his dad walked into the room, waving his hand in front of his nose.

"How many times have I told you to take that shit outside?" Pan asked irritably.

Brutus started laughing. "Relax, old man! I'm just unwinding. Been a crazy week, you know what I'm saying?"

Pan glared at Brutus for a moment before he burst out laughing and took off his hat, sitting down next to Brutus. "I know exactly what you mean, son."

"Between Mama becoming a yuppie and Cali's emotions getting outta control..."

"Tell me about it," Pan agreed as he cracked open and nursed a beer.

Soon, one beer turned into three as they began to partake in a drunken conversation. "You know, as much of a pain in the ass you are, you've always been my favorite, Brutus," Pan said.

"Aww shucks, old man!" Brutus laughed, looking at the

ceiling. "I figured it would be Julius! He was always more well-behaved. And he definitely does better in school than me."

"True, but at least you're a man, you know?" Pan scoffed, patting his chest. "Julius too much of a damn sissy for me! Boy's scared of his own uncle for god's sake."

Brutus turned to look back at him and cracked a nervous laugh. "That's with good reason though, Pops."

Pan chuckled. "The way I see it: you act like a bitch, you get treated like one. Julius was always too sensitive for me as a boy. Was more interested in watching the women cook than playing football or basketball with his cousins. As far as I'm concerned, what happened to him was a necessary evil. The boy needed to man up!"

"I ain't too sure about that, old man. Uncle Posei just infected Julius with the virus. I mean, dude got a boyfriend now and everything," Brutus blurted out nonchalantly, taking another sip of beer.

"What was that!?" Pan asked forcefully.

Brutus choked on his beer when he saw his dad wasn't amused. He patted himself on the chest and began to backtrack. "What was what?"

Pan's eyes glowered as he sat up on the couch. "Did you just tell me that your brother is another man's bitch!?"

Seeing his anger, Brutus's eyes enlarged as he further backtracked. "Ummm, did I say boyfriend? I meant to say *girlfriend*! I'm just too high right now!"

"Don't even try to play with me, Brutus! I heard what you said and you meant it!" Pan shouted. "I was already suspicious of his new friend anyway. Are they here right now?!"

"I... um... I mean..." Brutus stammered as his face broke out into sweats.

"Cut the bullshit and answer me! NOW!"

Brutus gulped and closed his eyes before he answered hesitantly. "Yes, Dad. They're here."

Pan shook his head as he got out of his seat and marched up the stairs while Brutus helplessly looked on. There was no way to stop him. All he could do was stare powerlessly as a knot formed in his chest over what he had just done. He heard yelling a few minutes afterward and ran up the stairs towards Julius's room. Calliope, Isis and Atum were all standing in the doorways of their rooms, eyeing the commotion unfolding in the hallway. Brutus paused a few feet behind Pan, with Julius and Pothos both shooting angry glares at him.

"THIS IS ALL YOUR FAULT!" Pothos yelled, lunging at Brutus before Julius held him back.

"Brutus is not the one in the wrong here," Pan asserted coldly. "You're the one in the wrong for perpetuating a lifestyle of sin! As are you for giving in so easily, Julius,"

"Dad, that's still your son! Please don't do this!" Calliope exclaimed, fighting back tears.

"This doesn't concern you, Calliope!" Pan scolded before refocusing his attention on Julius. "As for you, I will not have the noble Thessaly name tainted by a sexual deviant! I hereby relinquish your ties to this house and exclude you from the family trust. As of this minute, you are disowned from the House of Thessaly. Pack up your things! I want you out of here by morning."

"Daddy, I can't believe you!" Isis shouted, slamming her door shut. Atum nodded in agreement before following suit while Calliope held her hand over her mouth and stared helplessly, with tears streaming down her face. Pan made his way back downstairs while Pothos embraced Julius in a hug with Calliope joining shortly afterward.

Brutus stared at them silently, a large mass forming in his throat as he became overwhelmed with guilt and shame over telling their father of the affair in an inebriated daze. Julius wiped the tears from his eyes and sniffled glaring at Brutus once more. He bolted towards him and delivered a punch to the face so hard, Brutus ended up on the floor with a bloody nose.

"Brother, please! I didn't mean for any of this to happen!" Julius was unmoved, refusing to even look back at him as he walked back into his room as Pothos gave Brutus a kick to the stomach and followed suit. Calliope stared at him blankly for a few seconds before shaking her head and running back into her room, slamming the door behind her.

Brutus remained on the floor quietly in the darkened hallway for several minutes. He didn't do anything about his bleeding nose. He was at a total loss for both words and actions.

"I deserved all of that," Brutus reflected, regretting his foolish words and actions for the first time in his life. "This really is all my fault,"

Searching For The Red Light

After a restless night, I looked over to my blinds as the sunlight began to peer in slowly through the cracks. It was a new day, but all I could think about was Julius. Disowned.

No longer allowed to claim the family name or fortune. Such a status attracted hardly any sympathy from most people in Atalan. Instead eyebrows were raised in shock, faces tensed in disgust, and mouths would ask, "What did you do?" A social outcast, forced into life as a Lesser. A mere step above being an Untouchable was all it was.

I continued to sulk in my bed, not even getting out of the covers when the blood orange light of dawn broke through the window. I tossed and turned, staring around my room until I heard a knock at my door.

"Who is it?"

"It's Julius," he said solemnly from the other side of the door. "I wanna say goodbye." I rushed out of my bed, opened my door and smashed into him for a hug. As I felt his embrace, I choked up and began to sob heavily.

Julius stooped down and wiped my face. "Cali, don't cry. I'm a big boy, I can take care of myself."

"But where will you even go?" I asked, continuing to sob.

"I'm gonna move in with Pothos at his place in Clayton. And from there, I'm gonna search for a job. It will all work out, I promise you," he said softly as he pulled me in for a tighter hug.

"Stay in touch, will ya?"

"I don't think it would be a good idea for me to call. But I'll write you letters when I can."

"I'm gonna miss you, Julius."

"I'll miss you more." He picked up his bags and made his way down the hall.

I watched him until he reached the stairs. The minute he was no longer in my sight, I shut my door, ran to my bed and buried myself under the sheets and into the pillows once more.

* * *

Brutus laid in his bed, listening quietly as Julius knocked on the doors in the hallway and said his goodbyes to each of his siblings. He heard Julius talking to Calliope while she cried. He walked over to the door and placed his ear against it, hearing Julius say, "I'll miss you more" before walking away.

A large lump formed in his throat as he heard Julius's footsteps, hoping he'd knock. Instead, he heard the footsteps come and go. He opened his door to peer out and saw Julius making his way down the stairs. His eyes began to well up at the sight.

He closed his door and sat down on his bed, holding his face in his hands. *I just lost my brother. And I have no one to blame for it but myself*, he thought to himself.

After re-gaining his composure, he walked down the stairs to the kitchen. He saw Isis and Atum sitting at the table with bowls of cereal.

"Hey kids," he said coyly, only for them to turn around and

look at him with disdain.

"I can't believe what you did," Isis said coldly before turning back around, while Atum didn't even say a word. He picked up his bowl of cereal and left the kitchen. Calliope walked in, giving the cold shoulder to Brutus.

"Hey Cali," Brutus said as she opened the fridge.

"I'm not speaking to you, Brutus," Calliope responded coldly, refusing to look at him.

Brutus's jaw dropped slightly upon hearing her cold words. As siblings went about their business, he was overcome with a degree of vulnerability he had never felt. It had never occurred to him how much trouble his big mouth could cause. And like a boomerang, it came back around to strike him. Hard.

* * *

After breakfast, I returned to my room and stayed there. I didn't bother going to work at The Cornucopia. I didn't want to bear witness to my mother talking to her new yuppie friends without a care in the world despite the fact that her eldest son had just been disowned. And I definitely didn't want to be anywhere near Brutus. The mere sight of his face caused my blood to boil over. In my solitude, the only thing that could help me cope was writing.

I always knew, that the family pig
would one day go too far,
with his personal brand of Latin.
It wasn't even a question of "if",
so much as "when."
But never did I think,
 that would end

with me losing a brother.
I'm not even sure,
if I understand.
How can a man's disgust,
eclipse his love for his brother?
How can a man's hatred,
eclipse his love for his son?
How can a woman's obsession with status,
make her forget that she's a mother?
To think they all have the audacity,
to call this mess a family,
when all it is, is a house,
and not a home.

It was probably the darkest poem I had ever written. With the exception of my eldest brother and my two younger siblings, the Thessaly name meant nothing to me. If I had ended up being disowned right that second, I wouldn't have cared. At least then, I could run back to Auburn and live with Herc, finding true freedom at long last. Anything was better than remaining committed to this farce of a family.

I put my notebook away and ran my fingers through my coils as my eyes became fixated on the box again. A strange urge came over me, as if I thought the box was trying to tell me something. I got out of bed and made my way to the box, when Mama barged through my door, fuming.

"WHY WEREN'T YOU AT WORK TODAY?"

"Because I'm upset," I answered sarcastically.

"Calliope, I'm Julius's mother. I'm just as upset about all of this as you are, but that doesn't mean the world stops turning," she retorted with a calm, highly smug tone.

"Yeah right, Mama! If anything, you're just upset that your

oldest son decided to live his life! After all, you've made it very clear that the status of the family name is more important to you than being a mother to your children!" I countered while wagging my finger at her. She clenched her teeth and gripped her purse as her eyes seethed with rage. I stood still with a slight simper on my face. I had called her out and I was not sorry. She glared at me angrily as I eagerly awaited her rebuttal. After several tense seconds, she just closed her eyes and exhaled.

"I'm done here, Calliope. No matter what, you just do not want to listen or understand. Don't bother coming to work at the café anymore. All I can do at this point is pray that you won't be led astray even further," she asserted before leaving.

That's your problem, not mine, I thought. I picked up the box and sat on the bed with it.

I opened it and saw yet another note folded on top. Upon unfolding it, all I could do was scratch my head. A passage in Latin, it read:

"*Ignis, possedi ardens! Age infantem ignis accendit! Sine tuo proxime ignis!*

Inter terra, aqua, ignis, et tempestate non ultimum hoc unum volo mecum obtestatus!

Sed inter omnia elementa, quia hoc fascinum coniungere!

Ignis, possedi ardens! Age infantem ignis accendit! Sine tuo proxime ignis!

Inter terra, aqua, ignis, et tempestate non ultimum hoc unum volo mecum obtestatus!

Sed inter omnia elementa, quia hoc fascinum coniungere!"

I had no idea what any of it meant, but the rhythm of the code stayed with me. I played it over and over again in my mind for a few minutes when I felt a grumble in my stomach. I made my way out of my room and down to the kitchen. Nighttime had fallen, so I turned the light on in the hallway. As usual, all the doors were closed, except for the bathroom and judging from the rotten egg-like odor emanating from it, it was clear Brutus had just finished taking care of some business in there.

"Won't even bother to spray or light a candle," I ranted, eyeing the unlit candle sitting on the bathroom counter. I reached for the door and saw the candle light up by itself out of the corner of my eye.

I flinched, pausing to stare for a moment as a coconut aroma began to emanate from it. The odor began to neutralize as I walked into the bathroom and stared at the candle. I felt like the candle was smiling gleefully, teasing me as it continued to flicker over the hot, melting wax.

I walked out of the bathroom. "Was it a ghost? Was it already lit? Or... did I just do that with *my mind*?"

* * *

With nothing but a robe adorning his freshly showered and oiled body, Pan emerged from the bathroom of the motel room to the sight of his mistress waiting for him on the bed. Dressed in golden lingerie that fit tightly against her ivory skin, she reclined on the bed, with one hand in her strawberry-blonde hair and the other pressed provocatively against her thigh.

"I'm happy you decided to see me tonight, Theia," Pan said, disrobing as he steadily paced towards the bed. "I really needed this."

"Not a problem," Theia said, caressing the oily surface of his well-toned torso while looking up at him. "Must be tough finding out your son is the kind to get bent over, especially when you're the patriarch of a Noble house,"

"And that nagging, fat bitch of a wife just won't do," Pan said lustfully as he stared intently into her bright jade eyes. Theia pulled Pan down for a deep, passionate French kiss. He broke the kiss to ask a question. "Are you sure Odysseus doesn't know about our affair?"

"If he did, I'm sure he wouldn't care," she said breathily, pulling Pan in even closer. "He cheats on me all the time." They looked into each other's eyes longingly while they kissed. He laid in the bed next to her and started to fondle her body while she breathed heavily in silent anticipation. He removed her lingerie and pushed himself inside of her, setting off their evening liaison.

* * *

After another night of broken sleep, I awoke to a loud banging at my bedroom door. "Who is it?" I asked, irritated.

I heard my door open as I tilted myself up and turned to see Brutus walking into my room, holding the phone.

"I told you I wasn't speaking to you," I grumbled, glaring at him.

"I ain't gonna say a word to you. You got a phone call."

"From who?"

"Herc," he answered.

I hopped out of bed and yanked the phone out of his hand. I shooed him out of my room and shut the door, my eyes glowing with excitement.

"HERC!!!!" I enthused.

He returned the favor. "CALLIOPE!!!"

"How'd you find my phone number?" I asked.

"Because I'm like a ninja."

"How have you been?"

"Hanging in there. What about you?"

"Terrible. I've been arguing with Mama every day. My dad got us caught up with the Griffin Mafia. And two days ago, he disowned Julius."

Herc was silent for a moment. "What did Julius do?"

"He got into a new relationship..."

"So?"

"...with a man."

"Oh," Herc said, taking another pause. "Well, I mean-"

"Herc, please don't! I cried in my bed for hours after it happened. The last thing I need from you right now is a homophobic comment," I snapped.

"Well, let's just say I have my own feelings on that type of thing. I hate that your big bro had to go down like that. I'm truly sorry for you. Wish I could do something."

"Hearing your voice is enough," I said as a half-smile formed on my face.

"Have you made any friends out that way at least?"

"Only one. She's the daughter of one of the mob bosses. I can't stand the guy either. Or anyone else I've met around here. I'd rather just pretend these people don't exist."

"I'm not surprised. Griffin is not a place I'd ever step foot in if I could help it."

"Tell me about it," I said with a chuckle.

As we continued talking, I closed my eyes and pretended we were sitting on the grass in the Garden of Artemis, looking into his deep brown eyes with their copper shine while his dark skin glistened under the light of the summertime sun as kids laughed and played around us.

"Well, it's time for me to go," Herc said, killing the fantasy.

"I bid adieu to you Cali."

I choked up slightly. "Goodbye Herc. It was great to hear from you." He chuckled once more before the phone clicked away to the dial tone.

* * *

"They Reminisce Over You" by Pete Rock & C.L. Smooth played on the radio as Julius laid on the bed in Pothos's apartment, staring blankly at the ceiling and reminisced about his family. He thought of the days when Calliope, Isis and Atum were little, and he and Brutus would chase them around the house and make them laugh, waking up early in the morning and helping his mom do chores. Going to the barbershop with his dad.

He had positive things to think about each of his family members, even his father, despite being cruelly disowned by him. And yet, he had nothing but contempt in his heart for Brutus. Every time the image of his face came to mind, all Julius could think about was beating it to a pulp. Pothos walked into the room to let him know that lunch was ready, but he remained silent.

Pothos walked over to him and waved his hand over his face. "Everything alright with you, love?"

"I hate him," Julius replied, still fixated on the ceiling.

"You hate who?"

"Brutus," Julius said threateningly. "If I could kill him, I would!"

"Whoa Julius, now you know you don't really mean that!"

Julius sat up and looked at him with furrowed eyes. "Yes I do, Pothos. He's said and done some nasty things in the past, but I managed to forgive him every time. But this time, that motor mouth of his got me disowned from my house!"

"And the person who disowned you was Pan, not him," Pothos calmly interjected.

"Because Brutus told him to!"

Pothos rubbed his chin and looked away, briefly contemplating. "In the heat of the moment, I thought the same thing. But I'm starting to think that may not be the case. Did you see the look in his eyes? They weren't full of malice and contempt. They were full of concern and sorrow. You told me yourself he has a bad habit of not thinking before he speaks. Maybe he was talking to Pan and let it slip? I'm honestly starting to believe he didn't intend for any of that to happen."

Julius smacked his lips. "Yeah right."

Pothos leaned over with a soft smile. "Come on, baby. You don't think I know the feeling? My dad found out I was gay all the way back when I was thirteen. After that he forced me into a relationship with a girl. And believe me, I tried to make it work, but I knew who I was and didn't want to compromise. When I broke up with her a couple of months later, he disowned me."

Julius turned to look at him. "And what did you do?"

Pothos began to softly rub him on the head. "Well, the girl my dad made me date knew all along about who I really was. So when we went on dates, it was really just hanging out. Her family fell in love with me, and they didn't care about me being gay, so I just moved in with them. I guess I had it easy like that."

"Did you ever reconnect with your family?"

"I never lost touch with them in the first place. My mom loved me, no matter what. She tried to stop my dad, but he wasn't having it. My little brother was weirded out at first, but over time, he came to realize that my sexuality is only part of me. I have yet to make amends with my father, but if the opportunity shall ever arise, I will be more than happy to take it."

Julius began to weep uncontrollably. Pothos promptly embraced him in a hug. "You're a good person, Julius. Your family won't just forget you. It will all work out soon enough."

"Thanks for that," Julius said between his sobs. "I hope so too."

"Now come on, it's lunchtime! I made Cuban sandwiches."

"Do I look like I need to eat?" Julius asked, wiping his tears as he patted his belly.

"Everybody needs to eat!" Pothos said as he slapped his belly in reciprocation, before rubbing Julius's, as they made their way to the kitchen. "I love you just the way you are."

"How do you think your fam is holding up?" Pothos asked between bites of sandwich.

"My mom's too damn busy living a lie, so I ain't even worried about her. I know Isis and Atum are hurting, but I'm sure they'll be okay. I'm mostly worried about Calliope to be honest," Julius answered somberly.

"I can't help but to wonder what the deal is with her, man. You talked about how your parents kept her shut in for most of her life. And judging from her antics, it sounds like she doesn't even understand how Atalan works."

Julius put his sandwich down and leaned over to Pothos. "It's really complicated with her. I didn't think it was safe to tell you too much in our house, but now that they aren't around, I think now's the time I should start explaining."

Pothos sipped his cup of juice and gazed earnestly at Julius. "Go on."

"Well, for starters, she's not really my sister."

* * *

I walked downstairs in the middle of the night, only to see my mother laughing boisterously at *In Living Color* with a glass of red wine in her hand. It was the most jovial I had seen her in weeks. Instead of relief, I found myself dumbfounded as I walked over to her. "Mama, are you okay?"

"Never better, dearie!" she laughed, stumbling over her words in a drunken stupor. "All it took was some spirits to lift my spirits!" I stood there and stared at her for a moment, closing in on the wine glass, before I paced over and tried to grab it out of her hand.

She smacked it away before I could do so. "Have you lost your mind?!"

"Mama, I think you've had too many of those drinks."

She pursed her lips as she gave me a side-eye, while she poured herself another glass. "One too many?!" she replied, taking another swig. "Child, there is not enough wine in the world!"

I bit my lip and glared at her sadly, as she drank her sorrows away. She turned back to the TV and returned to her drunken laughing. I backed away ran up the stairs.

The red light. I had to see it.

When I reached the door to the roof-top balcony, I forcefully pushed it open and hurried up the next flight of stairs. I looked up at the sky, nary a star to be seen. Only ominous, dark red-violet shaded clouds framing a crescent moon. A sky that represented the passive rage I was feeling inside. I looked north towards the Atlantic Colony, trying to see the red light. I looked through miles and miles of the pitch black South Forest. In the far distance, I saw the city, but only in the form of a jumbled, nondescript string of lights and nothing more. There was no sign of what I beckoned for, the red light.

III

The New Normal

Adjust & Adapt

For several weeks in a row, I willfully imprisoned myself in my bedroom, leaving only to grab something from the kitchen or use the bathroom. I'd write until my hand ached. I listened to hip hop, new jack swing and g-funk so loud, people called the cops on us. Mama barged into my room to yell at me numerous times, but I really didn't give a damn. All I could think about was getting away. There were even a few occasions where I wished they'd just disown me already.

I laid in my bed as night had fallen, listening to footsteps in the hall provide an undertone to "Don't Sweat The Technique" by Eric B. & Rakim. My room was dark aside from a faint, red-tinted nightlight. I was on the verge of dozing off, when I heard a ball hit my window. I hopped out of bed and looked out, to see Fortuna standing there, laughing.

I smirked at her before opening the window. "What are you doing here?"

"I want to hang out!" Fortuna yelled with a smile and a shrug. "Feels like centuries since I've seen you!"

"Shh! Not so loud, you don't want my folks to hear you."

"Would you like to come hang out for a little bit?" Fortuna whispered loudly. "I stole my mom's car for the night!"

I was taken aback by her nonchalance in regards to stealing

her mother's car, but giggled. "I'd love to!"

I peered out my door to make sure no one was stirring, before quietly walking out of my room, down the stairs and grabbing the spare house key. By the time I made it to the driveway, Fortuna had already started up the bright yellow, well-maintained 1960's era Lincoln Continental.

Fortuna stuck out her hand to motion me over to the car. "Come on, Calliope!"

I laughed as I ran over to get in the passenger seat, glancing up at my house to make sure no one was looking out of the windows. Once I was strapped in, she pulled out of the driveway.

"So, how are you adjusting?" Fortuna asked, focused squarely on the road ahead.

"It's a struggle, but I'm making it work, I guess," I answered solemnly.

"I can only imagine. I heard about your brother getting disowned."

"Yeah, it's been tough," I replied, playfully twisting my curls in my fingers. "I'm so worried about him."

"Have you been able to stay in touch with him at least?"

"He said he'd write me letters, but it's been a month and I have yet to see one."

"I really do hope he's okay, 'cuz when you get disowned, everything about this city changes."

"I know. I don't even wanna think about what he could be going through right now to be honest," I added.

My heart skipped a beat as as we pulled up in front of The Cornucopia on Ponos Street. With my eyes furrowed, I turned to Fortuna. "Wait, why are we here?"

"Relax girl. We're just going to hang out on the rooftop at my dad's place across the street," Fortuna assured, flipping her hair back and getting out of the car.

I followed suit with a sliver of doubt. A lump in my throat formed as I thought about why we'd be going there of all places. I actually went so far as to think Fortuna set me up as the next casualty of the Griffin Mafia as she dug into the pocket of her ripped jeans to pull out the keys to Cicero's pizza shop. Once she opened it, she walked in and held the door for me to follow, but I couldn't help but to pause and stare like a deer in headlights.

"You're coming, right?" Fortuna asked with a raised eyebrow.

"I don't really know about this."

"I'm not a vampire in secret," she sarcastically retorted, "Besides, if that were the case you wouldn't have even met me yet!"

"You do like to hide from the sun a lot," I joked.

Fortuna rolled her eyes. "Don't be ridiculous! Now come on!"

I laughed nervously as she held the door open for me and we walked in. Aside from a faint light in the kitchen, the pizzeria was totally dark. I wasn't usually afraid of the dark, but something about the place gave me the creeps.

"Hungry?" Fortuna asked, making her way towards the refrigerator.

"A little bit."

"Let's dig into some pizza!" she exclaimed, pulling out a halved pizza, wrapped in aluminum foil and two sodas from the fridge. We sat at one of the red-and-white tablecloth covered tables, unwrapped the pizza and dug in.

"For future reference, the cooks here can make a decent pie, but it's not always fresh," Fortuna informed me, taking a swallow of soda. "My dad makes them wrap up whatever hasn't been served each night, so it can be reheated and served the next day. He's cheap like that."

"I can tell. It's not bad though," I said, taking another bite.

Fortuna gave a slight nod and raised her eyebrow. "Are you okay, Calliope?"

I shook my head and took a swallow of soda. "Yeah, I'm fine. Why do you ask?"

"Ever since we walked in, it's like you've been spooked by something."

"Well, I'm not." I shrugged my shoulders with a laugh, although, there was something about the place I found very unsettling.

Fortuna smiled slyly and leaned toward me. "Do you wanna hear an old urban legend about this place?"

"Sure," I answered confidently, gulping discreetly.

"You know about the Rupture of 1977, right?"

I paused. My mind flashed back to the diary entry I had read several weeks before. Just the mere reference sent chills up and down my spine.

"A little," I answered, nonchalantly.

"Rumor has it, the Crimson Maiden was killed in the room above us."

"Who's the Crimson Maiden?"

Fortuna laughed. "How could you know about the Rupture of 1977 without knowing about the Crimson Maiden? She was the main witch everybody was searching for after The Oracle!"

The box finally began to make more sense for me. The disappearing notes. The term "our kind." The fire incident. The mysterious passage in Latin. It was all about witchcraft. Strangely enough, all I wanted to do was learn more.

"Why was everyone after her?"

"It was over a bunch of different shit, but mostly it was because she messed with the Peloponnesians. And you *DON'T* mess with the Peloponnesians."

"How exactly did she 'mess' with them?"

"They say she went to one of the parties and conjured a 'disaster charm' or some voodoo crap like that. It made the chandelier fall and kill several guests."

My eyes grew wide and I practically shouted. "Oh my god! Why would she do that!?"

Fortuna placed her finger over her lips. "Shhhhh! Not so loud! Anyway, there's a number of rumors that went around. Some say that whole Resistance going on in the 70s ordered her to do it to scare Royals. Others say that Zeu-se raped her and she wanted revenge. There's also a few who said it never even happened. It's all nuts either way."

"Damn," I said with shocked eyes.

"Pretty intense, huh? Under Odysseus's orders, Atalan went open season on witches for six months. They'd banish you, throw you in The Dungeon or even kill you, if someone accused you of practicing magic. They were looking for the Crimson Maiden to turn herself in, but she completely disappeared. After the city was practically destroyed, everyone gave up searching for her."

"Where did the rumor about her being killed here come from?"

"People claimed they spotted her wandering around Griffin several months later," Fortuna explained, taking another bite of pizza and wiping her cheek. "But those were the last sightings of her ever reported. On the second floor of this building, there used to be a torture chamber. The Mafia used to fuck people up in there all the time. Makes a lot of sense when you put two and two together."

I gulped. "Damn."

"I know, right?! My dad owns this shop and even he's afraid to go to the second floor," Fortuna said, taking another sip of soda. "Wanna go to the roof for a smoke when we're done eating?"

I stopped mid-bite to stare at her. Going up on the roof meant we would have to walk through the second floor. The mere thought of it terrified me.

Fortuna shrugged with a smile. "You're staring at me like I just spoke a foreign language to you."

I swallowed my food. "After what you just said, this building just freaks me out too much to want to go any further."

"Oh come on, you scaredy-cat!" Fortuna teased. "I do it all the time!"

I sat back and looked around before I shook my head and obliged. We finished up our pizza and sodas before we made our way to the roof.

We walked towards the door in the back, which revealed a dusty, creaky old staircase. The room above was almost completely dark aside from the street lights emanating a faint glow through the windows. Fortuna started to make her way up the staircase. I gulped before following suit, a strong chill running down my spine when I heard the door slam shut by itself behind us. When we made it to the top of the stairway, I was surprised at the sight of numerous, dusty devices, still sitting around in ominous repose.

I paused to observe the room. Between the rusty shackles on the metal bed of a stretching machine, the rack of hanging, bloodied razor blades and the tall, skinny incinerator standing in the middle of the room which smelled like death itself, the entire room was a morbid sight to behold.

I looked towards the other end of the room, to be met with the most frightening sight of all. It was a giant wheel, like the kind that can be found at a circus or carnival. However, this wheel was covered in giant blood stains. I felt a stabbing pain in my chest when my eyes first gazed upon it, as if I had been strapped to the wheel myself while a demented carnie spun me around as oblivious children laughed, trying their luck with flying daggers.

"Calliope?"

I blinked quickly and shook my head to snap myself out of the daze. "Yes?"

"You're looking at the wheel, aren't you?"

I nodded my head. "That thing always did give me the creeps. And I'm pretty hard to scare. Come on, let's get out of here and go up on the roof."

She motioned for me to follow her through a dark, dusty doorway which held another set of stairs. At the top of the staircase was a door that opened to the roof. She held it open for me as I followed. On the rooftop were three reclining lawn chairs. She offered me a cigarette and the two of us sat on the lawn chairs to talk underneath the starlight.

* * *

"Oh my god! Oh my god! My dad is gonna be so mad if he finds out about this!"

"You better quiet down then, girl. Shit!"

Brutus had snuck into the bedroom of the girl next door. Medea's dark blonde hair flew around all over the place, while her green eyes fought to stay open as Brutus thrusted himself inside her pale, slender body.

Brutus huffed and puffed as she tried her best to have a quiet orgasm. They were both caught off guard when she unleashed a shrill scream.

"Shit!" Brutus exclaimed quietly as heavy footsteps began to pound down the hallway. Medea, trying to regain her breath and composure, motioned for him to move off of her and hide. He pulled out, rolled out of the bed and hid underneath a blanket as her father violently opened the door to her room.

"MEDEA!"

"Yes?!" she asked shakily, sitting up in the bed.

"Why were you screaming?"

"I just had a really bad nightmare, that's all," Medea answered nervously as Brutus sweated away underneath the blanket he was hiding under, almost blue in the face from holding his breath.

Medea's father paused for a moment, staring at his daughter with eyes widened in disbelief. "I could have sworn I heard another voice coming from this room."

"I'm not sure what you're talking about. It was just another nightmare about my ex-boyfriend beating me up."

Medea's father scoffed. "How many times do I have to tell you I don't believe that damn lie?!"

Medea groaned. "Just because I didn't have any bruises doesn't mean it didn't happen!"

"I'm going back to bed. Hope your next dream is a sweet one," he said, closing her door.

Brutus took a loud gasp of breath as Medea patted him on the back. "I thought he'd never leave. I think I recognize that voice though."

Medea stood in a pink t-shirt and nothing else. "Do you really?"

"Ain't he the big boss at that club the Griffin Mafia be hangin' out at?"

"The Megalopolis?"

"Yeah, that one."

"That's correct," Medea replied. "He's Mr. Phil, owner of The Megalopolis and high-standing Griffin Mafia associate."

Brutus chuckled. "God damn! Wait til' I tell people I boned his daughter!"

"You don't want to tell anyone about this. My dad would try to kill me if he found out. Especially if he knew I did it with someone like you."

Brutus tilted his head dumbfounded. "Someone like me? What the hell is that supposed to mean?"

Medea threw her hands up. "Someone Black!"

Brutus gulped nervously. "It's that serious, huh?"

"Yeah, it is! So take a chill pill and keep it shut!"

Brutus chuckled and smiled. "Wanna go for round two then?"

Medea rolled her eyes. "After my dad almost caught us? No, we can do this another night. Now go back home!"

Brutus scoffed. "I see how it is." He put some of his clothes back on and quietly climbed out her window.

* * *

I don't know what time it was when Fortuna dropped me off at home. I let out a sigh as I said goodbye and made my way back into the house. After numerous weeks trapped within the walls of a prison of bad memories and experiences, spending time outside with a friend was a breath of fresh air. It reminded me of the good old days with Herc, minus the creepy surroundings. I didn't mind having a laugh and smoke with Fortuna, but everything else about the building was far too unsettling. The bad memories held within that place were overwhelming.

As I paced down the cobblestone walkway to the front door, I looked down and contemplated why it had such a profound effect on me. I could legitimately feel my insides churn as I laid my eyes upon the wheel. I felt terrified, sick, and sad. Sad enough to cry. It was as if I had a connection I wasn't aware of.

"Cali?" I heard someone whisper behind me.

I turned around to see Brutus, wearing nothing more than a black wifebeater and boxers, holding a pair of jeans in his arms.

"Brutus?!" I asked with a perplexed scowl. "What are you doing?"

"I could ask you the same thing. You ain't the goin' out type, especially not this late."

"For your info, I snuck out to hang with Fortuna. Why the hell are you wandering around half-naked outside our house at this time of the night?"

Brutus let out a laugh. "The same reason a lot of other people are naked at this time of night."

"I should have figured."

"You walked right into that one, sis," Brutus joked with a slightly awkward laugh.

"Apparently," I coolly replied, making my way back to the door, preparing to unlock it.

"Hey Cali, can I talk to you?"

"No. I'm still mad at you."

"Come on, sis. Just hear me out at least!" Brutus quietly exclaimed, throwing his hands up.

I put my hand on my hip and tilted my neck. "Hear you out on what? That you hate your brother?"

Brutus paused for a moment with his mouth slightly agape. "I don't hate him. I can't believe you think I do."

"What am I supposed to think!? He was disowned because of you!"

He nodded his head. "I know." He closed his eyes, looked

down and began to cry. "None of it would have happened if I didn't open my damn mouth!" he said between sobs.

My jaw dropped at the sight of the invincibly obnoxious, insensitive Brutus, crying like a puppy. I couldn't help but to be sympathetic. I walked over to him for a hug before we made our way back inside the house, deciding that I would oblige his request to hear his side of the story after all.

The Whole Story

"So you never meant for any of it to happen?"

"I swear to you," Brutus said with sincerity as he put his hand on his chest. "Cross my heart."

I paused and twiddled my fingers for a moment. "Okay, I believe you. But for you to just let it slip out to Dad like that–"

"I was high and drunk! Ever since it happened, I keep playing the same scenario in my head, thinking to myself: what if I just took my blunt and bottle to my room? Or to the pool? Or just wasn't smoking or drinking at all? That conversation would have never happened and Julius would still be with us. I don't even care about who he's getting down with anymore, I just want my brother back!" Brutus fought back another round of tears.

My heart sank as I saw Brutus break down and cry. For the first time ever, I had seen his heart. And it was hurting.

I scooted closer to him on the couch and patted him on the back. "It's not your fault. You shouldn't blame yourself."

"Yes it is!" Brutus said, placing his face in his hands and continuing to sob. "Julius got disowned because of me!"

"Julius promised he would send me a letter one day. I don't know when it's gonna come, but I'll be sure to explain everything in my reply. I'm sure he'll forgive you."

Brutus sniffled and regained some of his composure, shaking his head. "No, he won't. I don't think he ever will."

"We both know how Julius is! It's not in his nature to stay angry and hold grudges."

Brutus turned to look at me with vacant eyes. "That's how he is with everyone except me."

* * *

Dear Cali,

First off, I'd like to give you an apology for not writing to you sooner. I know you've been really worried about me, but just know that I'm okay now. I can't say that I've completely healed from what happened just yet. I still cry myself to sleep over it sometimes. Don't even know any words to express how much I miss seeing you, Isis and Atum's faces. I expected to leave the nest sooner or later, just can't believe it had to happen the way it did.

I'm still looking for a job, but everything's been good with me and Pothos.. He keeps me going these days. Feel free to stop by whenever you like.

With warm love and regards,

Julius

P.S. Tell everyone I said hi. Well, everyone except for Dad and Brutus.

"Don't you think you could leave that last part out? Seems kinda mean."

Julius turned around to see Pothos looking over his shoulder.

"Mean? I ain't about to act like I wanna see or talk to them when I know damn well I don't."

"Julius, you can't hold a grudge forever!"

Julius stroked his goatee. "You gonna try and tell me I have no right to be mad at them?"

Pothos threw his head back in frustration. "Ugh! Are we really gonna have this conversation again?"

Julius let out a brief chuckle before he stood up from his chair, pulling Pothos in for a kiss. "How about we have another session instead?"

Pothos pushed him away. "No thanks. Your childishness is a total turn-off for me."

Julius shrugged and threw his hands up. "And you acting like a queen turns me off!"

Pothos, who was making his way back to the room, turned around with a sly smile. "I wasn't the queen when I turned the tables the other night."

"Man, shut up!" Julius responded angrily, furrowing his eyebrows with cheeks slightly red.

"And I'm the one being a queen right now," Pothos said with a laugh.

Julius scoffed and shook his head. He looked over his letter again. After several minutes, he sighed and crossed out the offending line. He placed the letter in an envelope and put it in the mail drop, but not before adding one more line: "*P.S.S. Cali, if Brutus wants to talk, then by all means, let me know.*"

* * *

Golden rays of light broke through the living room curtains as my eyes slowly broke open and I looked at the clock to see it was 5:45 A.M. I started to yawn when I noticed that I was laying on Brutus's shoulder. To my surprise, I couldn't help but kiss him on the cheek and warmed up to see him smile a little bit in his sleep. He had been in a really lonely place and seeing that he was not the hateful monster I thought he was, I felt that he deserved to know love from someone.

As he continued to sleep, I made my way off the couch and started walking up the stairs. Thanks to Fortuna, the box was calling my name once more. Having made mental notes of the missing puzzle pieces revealed to me the previous night, I was anxious to read whatever scrap of paper was shown to me on top.

"Look who finally emerged from her slumber," Mama snidely remarked while shooting me an unfriendly eye, as I neared the top of the staircase.

I crossed my arms. "Good morning to you too, Mama." I walked past her and into my room, closing the door behind me. I bolted to the box, anxious to see what anecdote it had to offer me. As expected, another piece of folded red paper was on top. With my heart almost beating its way out of my chest, I unfolded it excitedly and began reading.

December 20th, 1976

The human heart can be a strange thing sometimes.

Mere days ago, I hated my older brother with every fiber in my being. His jealousy caused me to get disowned from my former house. But even before then, our sibling relationship was faltering thanks to his obsession with wealth and privilege, desires that are the complete opposite of mine. I was never on the same page with the so-called Nobles we grew up around in Auburn. I grew up to join the Atalan Resistance. He grew up to become a regular guest of honor at the Peloponnesian parties. Go figure.

And yet, today, my heart is aching for him. My good friend Hera told me that his wife gave birth to a baby girl who never woke up.

I couldn't help but to tear up when I heard the news. When I was disowned a year ago, I was so angry I conjured a curse of repetition on his two baby boys out of pure spite. The least I could do was reverse the curse on them, and I don't even know how to do that. Anger and impulse can be very scary things.

As I rub my belly, feeling the seed kicking within, the feeling is one of mortality. What if the same thing were to happen to me?

Scary as it seems and sick as I feel to even think of such a notion, perhaps it would be just as much a gift as it would be a curse. After all, with practitioners of magic, bearers of the aura and the two-natured being caught left and right and the Resistance becoming overly reckless with their moves, I can sense another rupture brewing.

Hecate Diner used to be the safest place in town for a Mage. It's where I found refuge after being disowned. Now, that's starting to not be the case. The status of safety was already complicated by the fact the diner is located in the Cascade, the most dangerous polis in all of Atalan. But now, there have been a number of watchers. I've carefully looked out the window at night over the past few weeks and witnessed men dressed in black suits observing the building, even stopping passersby to ask questions.

The other day, another man in a suit by the name of Hadrian, came to the diner and went on a full-blown tirade against witchcraft out of nowhere. Terpsi responded with a blank face and silence while me, Eros and Urania looked at him in shock. The incident was already suspicious enough, but for all of us to react the way we did, didn't do much to help preserve our cover.

As if that wasn't scary enough, we have a serial killer on the loose that appears to be targeting those who've committed sins. His most recent victims were a teenage boy and girl having sex in a car. The car was tagged: "Thou Shalt Not Consummate Without Marriage." If that's how he feels about sex before marriage, then lord knows what he would think of the Magic class or any other Mystic.

So much going on right now, I can't help but to feel selfish for *bringing a child into this world.*

I gulped as I finished reading the note and put it away. I thought the conversation I had with Fortuna the night prior would help me gain a better understanding of the notes in the box, but I was left with even more questions.

The Hera I knew of was Zeu-se's wife, the current matriarch of the House of Peloponnesian. I couldn't comprehend the thought of a Peloponnesian willfully keeping the company of someone who was either a Lesser or a witch, let alone both.

The "curse" sounded eerily similar to the situation between Julius and Brutus. Not to mention, the biblical serial killer she alluded to. Everything about the box got more bizarre and complex each time I opened it. I was beginning to wonder how much did I really knew about Atalan.

* * *

Demeter beamed with joy as she bore witness to the packed Cornucopia. The line was out the door. Every table was occupied. Pastries were flying off the shelves as Isis and Atum worked at top speed, with general consensus being they were more pleasant than Calliope and Brutus.

"Here's your espresso, Mr. Cicero." Isis said cheerfully as she handed him his coffee cup. "Dark with a thin layer of foam, just how you like it."

Cicero nodded. "You're doing a great job, young lady. Thank you for that."

Isis smiled and made her way back to the kitchen, before Demeter stopped her. "Good job Isis. You're much better at aiming to please than your siblings."

Isis awkwardly chuckled, side-eyeing her as she walked back

into the kitchen. Demeter didn't appear to notice, pleased with how enthusiastic Atum was greeting and serving each customer. When things began to slow down, she proceeded to sit with two unlikely new friends, Cicero and Romulus.

"I have to say, things have really improved around here since you got rid of those two rebels," Cicero enthused, taking another puff of his cigar.

Demeter smiled and laughed. "Tell me about it."

"The only thing we gotta worry about now is getting AIDS," Romulus joked. "The fact that homo brother of theirs was touching these cups has me shook."

The three of them burst into a fit of laughter, with Demeter laughing awkwardly. Time whizzed by as they proceeded to talk about business, while Isis looked on drearily as Atum shook his head.

* * *

"Aw come on, Cali. Why I gotta be a pig?"

"It was the analogy that made the most sense at the time," I said nonchalantly as he read poems I wrote in my notebook. We stared at each other for a moment before bursting out laughing. As "Tennessee" by Arrested Development played in the background, I was enjoying the newfound bond I was making with Brutus.

For the past two days, we had kept each other company and loved every minute of it. Truth be told, our distaste for one another could have been rooted in the fact that we really didn't know each other to begin with. Over those two days, we shared our interests and vulnerabilities with one another, he started to appear more human and I started to appear like less of a weirdo.

Our conversation was so refreshing, I almost forgot the lingering smell of weed in his room.

"Yo, sis, you sure you don't want a hit of this?" he asked, offering his pungent blunt to me.

"Yeah, I'm sure," I politely refused, softly pushing his hand away.

He shrugged and smiled. "More trees for me." He took another hit, subtly coughing afterward.

"Brutus, why did you use to hate me so much?"

He stopped mid-laugh and stared at me for a couple seconds. "I don't hate you. I never did."

"You sure did act like it."

"I know," he said indifferently, slowly nodding his head and taking another hit of his blunt before putting it out.

"But the question is *why* though? I mean, now I see that you aren't... *completely* terrible, so why have you only shown your terrible side to me in the past?"

"It was jealousy."

"You were jealous of me?" I asked in wide-eyed disbelief. "Please explain."

"I felt like you got in the way of me and Julius. I don't remember a whole lot from before then, but I remember that me and him were peas in a pod. Once you came though, he was always babying you and that took attention away from me."

"You've never been mean to Isis and Atum."

"I was a little jealous of them too, but it was kinda different with them, you know?"

"Different how?"

"I mean, a little sister and little brother are one thing, but an adopted cousin? Whole 'nother ballpark right there," he said with a straight face.

My mouth hung open like a codfish as my heart dropped. "Excuse me!?"

"What?" Brutus asked nonchalantly.

"I'm not your sister?"

"I thought Julius told you that a long time ago?"

I scowled my eyes at him and shook my head before leaving his room.

I heard Brutus call out behind me, but I was so offended I didn't even care. "Aww now, come on! It don't mean we don't love you Cali," I walked over to my room and shut the door behind me.

The Dream

My eyes opened to pitch-black nothingness. My sight was clouded with a bizarre haze as I began to look around. I heard a piercing scream followed by a combination of multiple voices laughing and crying simultaneously. I heard tambourines and cymbals and saw a woman emerge from the haze.

She was tall and skinny with mahogany skin, completely nude from head to toe. Her head was shaking so quickly, I couldn't make out her face. The sobs and laughter became louder and louder, joined by a piercing, tortured scream.

All of the noises were coming from her. I covered my ears and winced as she moved closer to me. My eyes bulged and my teeth chattered as my body froze. I was mortified, but I couldn't move. When she was right in front of me, she stopped in her tracks and her face became still.

She was practically a clone of me, with deep brown eyes, a wide nose and plump lips with a diamond-shaped face. Her hair was also just like mine, a mane of long, tight and curly black coils. Her face was scowled at first, but relaxed into a smile as she reached up and took my hands off my ears.

"Calliope!" she enthused. "You've lived the lie for far too long! Wake up to the truth!"

I gasped for air as I sat up quickly and opened my eyes. I looked around my room and everything appeared to be normal. Rays of sunlight burst through the blinds as I wiped the cold sweat off my face and pondered the dream I had.

I looked at my dresser and saw the box.

I pulled off the sheets, paced towards the dresser and opened the box to see what it would reveal. I was welcomed to another folded piece of paper on top; however, unlike prior notes, this one was purple. Something about it struck me as eerie and disconcerting. I glanced at it with unease for a moment before I unfolded it and began reading.

Dear Calliope,

I can breathe a sigh of relief now that I have finally found you, after so many years of searching. Seeing that nothing went to plan, we have about fourteen years worth of things to talk about. I have no idea where to even begin, so I feel it would be best to let you ask the first question. But be quick, another rupture is brewing in Atalan, and where you live is the nucleus of it. You finding this box was no accident. The key to your destiny is held within. I can tell you're a very smart girl, so I'm sure you'll figure out how to reply to this letter.

Til' we speak again,

The Oracle

A cold wind ran up and down my spine as I threw the note back into the box, snapped it shut and backed away. I had only started to figure out who The Oracle was, and yet, she had been searching for me since I was a baby?

And how did that letter even get there? Surely, she couldn't have been stalking me over the past couple of weeks, to find some way to sneak into my room undetected. As my mind was racing, I heard someone knock on the door. Startled, I flinched.

"Who is it?" I asked shakily.

"It's Brutus," he said, opening my door and stepping in anyway.

I relaxed, but only a little. "What is it this time?"

Brutus let out a chuckle and smirked. "Really, sis? You're already back to thinking I'm a pain in the ass?"

"I didn't appreciate what you said yesterday."

His smirk went away before he nodded. "I know. It was wrong for me to tell you like that, but you know how I am when I'm high."

I crossed my arms, gave a sigh and rolled my eyes.

"I have a surprise for you!" He held one of his hands behind his back before revealing a letter.

I rushed over and took the letter out of his hand. I saw it was from Julius and let out a quick yelp.

"I know there ain't anything nice for me in there, so I'll go now," Brutus said with a deflated smirk, before I stopped him.

"We won't know until we open it. Come on and read it with me!"

We sat down on my bed and gave his letter a thorough read. I was so happy to know that he was okay and that Pothos was helping him cope. Brutus started to tear up when he was finished.

"He doesn't hate me," Brutus said, wiping his eyes and pointing at the last line.

"Oh my god, this is wonderful! You can explain yourself and open up the opportunity for forgiveness!"

Brutus let out a chuckle. "Yeah. Question is, how are we gonna go about that?"

"Simple, we just go to his new place. He said we can stop by whenever we like," I suggested enthusiastically.

"No, *YOU* can stop by," Brutus said, his voice and expression hardening up. "Didn't say anything about me."

"I'm not sure I understand."

Brutus looked away and walked out of my room. "Maybe it's not time for you to understand."

I paused and stared at the letter, still in hand. I couldn't help but to ponder his strained relationship with Julius. It was becoming clear that the rift between the two started long before Brutus outed him.

* * *

"Fortuna, even as I talk to you, you still seem like such an enigma to me!"

"I know, but I can already see that we're going to make great friends, Cali! Just give me a little more time to unravel, okay?"

Fortuna smiled as she laid in bed, listening to "Come As You Are" by Nirvana, thinking of the conversation she had on the roof of her dad's pizza shop with Calliope several nights prior. They related to each other over their stressful home lives. Fortuna talked about Pietas and laughed when Calliope winced after asking her if she ever thought about boys. She gave her more advance warnings over what things were like at Pegasus High. Her stomach was turning at the thought of returning to school there in less than a week.

"Ugh, why am I only a junior?" Fortuna said to herself with angst, getting out of bed and walking downstairs to the kitchen. "I can't stand the thought of another year at that place!"

She walked past the black and white photos Cicero referred to as the family dynasty down the marble staircase. She looked around the brightly lit foyer with indifference as she made her way to the kitchen where she was greeted to the sight of the family maid. Syne was a short, copper-skinned, full-figured woman in her early 60s with salt-and-pepper hair, styled into a long bob. She hummed away as she prepared the morning breakfast spread.

Her mother Tyche sat at the rectangular kitchen table, nursing a cup of coffee. Her cold, blue eyes stared emptily into space, pursing her lips after each sip as she repeatedly fluffed her pin-curled blonde hair. Fortuna rolled her eyes and deliberately ignored her.

"Good morning, Syne," she said cheerfully as she picked up a plate.

Syne turned to her with a smile. "Good morning to you too, Fortuna! I made brown sugar waffles."

"My favorite!" Fortuna put two of them on her plate and drizzled them with molasses before picking up a fork and heading back to her room.

"I'm happy you acknowledged my presence this morning, daughter," Tyche said snidely.

Fortuna paused and turned around to look at her, bemused. "Good morning."

She continued to make her way out of the kitchen, as Tyche scowled her eyes and halted her. "No, Fortuna! I would like to talk to you!"

Fortuna turned around and stared at her silently. She rolled her eyes and reluctantly obliged, sitting at the far end of the table, deciding it would be best to deal with her mother's nonsense quickly.

"Would you rather I excuse myself?" Syne nervously asked.

Tyche shot her a cold stare before lighting a cigarette. "You're excused."

"Yes ma'am," Syne said with a nod as she made her way out of the kitchen.

Tyche focused her attention back to Fortuna. The two of them made silent eye contact for almost a minute before Fortuna gave another eye roll, shrugged her shoulders and started to eat her waffles.

"So late-night joyrides are your new thrill now, huh?"

Fortuna's eyes grew big as she almost choked on a piece of waffle. She gave a quick pound to her chest to make sure she didn't choke, before quickly chewing and swallowing her food to muster her response. "What was that?" she asked with feigned confusion.

Tyche took another puff of her cigarette as she stood up from her chair and started to laugh. "Don't try to act like you don't know what I'm talking about."

"I really don't know," Fortuna said with shrugged shoulders, continuing to feign ignorance before taking another bite of her waffle.

"Oh, really? Then explain this!" Tyche exclaimed as she opened one of the cupboards in the kitchen, with a TV and VCR inside. She turned on the TV, and showed a videotape of her in the garage a couple of nights before, getting in her mother's car and driving off with it. Fortuna's jaw dropped at the footage while Tyche stared at her with a maniacal smile.

"How did you get that?!"

"You're so bad at listening and paying attention, I figured you wouldn't notice the new cameras I installed which detail your every move."

"This is a joke, right!?"

"It's not a joke at all, dear. Now I know what that second shower is all about. You run the hot water just so you can get away with taking a hit of your water pipe. No wonder your eyes are always so red when you're done."

Fortuna raised her eyebrow and asked, "Wait. You keep a video camera *in my bathroom?*"

Tyche laughed again. "And your bedroom, too. That boyfriend of yours, what's his name? Pie-toes? Doesn't seem too good in bed, now does he?"

Fortuna gulped as she stared at her mother with wide eyes. She got out of her seat and went back to the breakfast spread to pour herself a glass of orange juice.

"I've rendered you speechless." Tyche remarked contemptuously with a smirk.

Fortuna took a sip of her orange juice, still looking down at the spread. "Okay, I may not get along with my dad, but we can agree on one thing: you are one crazy bitch."

Tyche laughed again and shook her head as she poured herself a glass of orange juice. She took a flask from another cabinet and mixed it in, stirring with her finger. "After all these years of being called that, I've learned to take it as a compliment."

Fortuna shook her head. "That's exactly why I'm ashamed to call you my mother." She left the kitchen, with her orange juice and plate of waffles in hand, and went back upstairs to her bedroom.

* * *

I was in the midst of writing my response letter to Julius when I heard someone knock on my door. I got off my bed and was greeted to the sight of Isis and Atum.

"Hey, you two!" I greeted enthusiastically. I could tell by their vacant eyes that all wasn't well with them. "How is everything?"

Isis sighed. "Not too great." Atum shook his head. I sighed and invited them into my room to talk.

"This is about The Cornucopia, huh?"

"You guessed it," Atum said, attempting to be humorous, but the vacancy in his face and voice buried any possible comedy.

I nodded my head. "So what's been going on?"

Isis twiddled her fingers. "Well, it's not that we don't mind working there. It's kind of fun actually. The thing that's getting us is... well, Mama's really changed."

"I see, go on," I asserted, even though I already kinda figured what was up.

"She's pretty much best friends with those Godfather guys now," Isis continued.

"They also badmouth you, Julius and Brutus all the time," Atum added. "She never even bothers to defend you guys. She just laughs,"

I let out a chuckle. "Yeah, I saw that when I was working there. Tell me something I don't know."

Isis and Atum both glanced at each other solemnly before Atum turned to me. "I think Cicero's trying to tear the family apart."

My eyes grew wide. "What makes you think that?"

"Yesterday, he said 'hey kid, don't be surprised if you get a new daddy soon,'" Atum mocked with his best imitation of Cicero's stereotypical Italian-American accent.

I paused in disgust, then closed my eyes and hugged both of them tightly. It was really all I could do.

* * *

Brutus stared silently at a piece of paper, slowly smoking

another blunt. As night fell, the only light in his room was the faint light over his desk. His stereo had been playing the whole time, but not a single song struck a nerve in him until "They Reminisce Over You" by Pete Rock and C.L. Smooth started playing and he began to weep, each tear hitting the paper with a soft thud.

"You just don't know how much I miss you, bro," Brutus said to himself, taking another hit off the blunt. Someone banged loudly at the door.

Brutus wiped his eyes and scowled, clearing his throat. "Who the hell it is!?"

"BRUTUS! OPEN YOUR DAMN DOOR NOW!"

"Oh shit!" Brutus exclaimed. He took one last hit before putting it out and searching frantically through his dresser for his bottle of air freshener. He quickly sprayed it around his room, the citrus aroma clashing chaotically with the marijuana smoke instead of covering it up. He regained his composure, with a fake smile as the cherry on top and opened his door.

"Hey Pops!" Brutus said with forced enthusiasm.

Pan stood at the doorway with scowled lips and glaring eyes, indicating that he wasn't amused. "How many times do I have to tell you to not smoke that shit in my house?"

Brutus let out an awkward smile as he flailed his arms. "Oh, that? I wasn't smokin' weed. I just let out a really bad fart!"

"Don't be gross," Pan scoffed.

"It's the truth!" Brutus joked, hoping it would cool Pan's temper. "Hot cheese and peppers on nachos can be a deadly combo, yo."

"I'm not in the mood for your crude sarcasm right now. Cicero, Romulus, Remus and I need you at the Megalopolis again. Tonight."

Brutus raised his left eyebrow. "Again? I actually have something really important to do right now."

"I don't care! Get your fat ass dressed!" Pan demanded. "I'll be waiting in the car." He made his way down the stairs, while Brutus looked on.

* * *

I stared into the hazy, violet dusk of the nothingness, laying there still, without so much as a peep. Looking all around, I couldn't help but shake the feeling of being watched. Out of nowhere, the figure appeared again. The same woman from the dream before. Fading in through the haze and growing steadily clearer, I bore witness to her deep brown eyes staring at me and into the depths of my soul.

"You should really answer that letter," she said firmly.

I almost smothered myself with my sheets, unraveling them off myself and sitting up in bed. I huffed and puffed as sweat rolled down my face and neck. I looked all around my darkened room, still feeling that I was being watched. I looked at my clock to see that it was 5:45 A.M. My eyes wandered to the box once more.

I wiped the sweat off my brow and brushed back the hair out of my face. "She's right, I should." I said, determined.

I got out of my bed and made my way to the box. I opened it, faced with the same purple note The Oracle had sent to me. I unfolded it and started writing on the other side, not entirely sure if it would work.

Dear Oracle,

This is Calliope. I'd like to apologize for my delayed response, I wasn't sure what to do. I barely know who you are or who this other

Calliope is. This box has given me many questions, few of which have been answered. I would deeply appreciate it if you could help me answer some of them. I only ask that we go at my own pace.

With curious sincerity,

Calliope

I finished my letter and placed it in the box when I heard someone open my door. I turned around, to see Brutus emerge from the other side. His eyes were dazed and catatonic, as he stumbled his way into my room. He was sweating profusely, and smelled like a freshly opened bottle of vodka. I couldn't tell if he was staring at me or just out into space before he collapsed onto my bed. I let out a slight gasp and ran over to him.

"Brutus, are you okay?" I asked, trying to hold him up. A second later, he vomited all over himself and my bed.

Clarity

A slender, big-haired Demeter was enjoying a drink with Aunt Circe, while Pan stood on the patio, enjoying a cigar with Uncle Posei. Atum was getting a kick out of his toy train, still in his pajamas, adorned with cartoon lions while Isis hummed away and decorated her new dollhouse. Meanwhile, Calliope's nose wouldn't budge from her new copy of *A Wrinkle In Time*. It was the day after Christmas 1985 and the holiday spirit was present as ever in the House of Thessaly.

Everyone in the room had a smile on their face except Brutus. He sulked, sitting in the recliner usually reserved for Pan. He looked around silently at everyone, his eyes furrowed into a disgusted glare as he closed in on Uncle Posei. Demeter and Circe stopped mid-laugh when they noticed how quiet he was.

"Brutus, is everything okay?" Circe asked, stirring her drink. "I've never seen you this quiet before."

"Someone must have taped his mouth shut," Calliope butted in, eyes still fixated on her book. "That's a good thing,"

"Now, now, Calliope, don't be rude," Demeter chided. "Brutus, your auntie is right. I don't think I've heard you say a single thing all day. You would think that'd be a relief, but this isn't like you. Something on your mind?"

Brutus looked at Demeter but just quietly shook his head. "It's nothing."

"Okay then," Demeter said with an unsure tone and worried eyes.

"May I be excused upstairs?" Brutus requested. Demeter, Circe and Calliope all stopped what they were doing and paused to look at him.

"Yes, you may," Demeter obliged, taking another sip of her drink, the worry in her eyes ever growing.

"Manners from Brutus?" Calliope remarked as Brutus got out of the chair and made his way upstairs. "I never thought I'd see the day," He gulped as he looked at the door to Julius's bedroom in the darkened hallway. He paced towards it slowly and knocked on the door with slight hesitation.

"Who is it?!" Julius shouted nervously from the other side.

"It's your bro," Brutus answered with an undertone of guilt.

There was an elongated silence before Julius replied. "Come in."

He opened the door and walked in, to see Julius laying on the bed with his back turned to him. Closed blinds and an overbearing grief shrouded Julius's room in impenetrable darkness.

"Are you feeling any better today?" Brutus inquired with uncertainty.

Julius sniffled with a cracked voice. "No."

"Is there anything I can do to help?" Brutus asked, scratching his back nervously.

Julius let out a chuckle between his sobs. "Why?! It ain't like you did anything to help last night!"

"Julius, please," Brutus pleaded, fighting tears himself.

"You let him do it!" Julius yelled, turning to him with puffy, bloodshot eyes. "You let him do that to me!"

"Julius, I didn't-"

"You just sat there and watched! You let it happen!"

"I didn't know what to do! You gotta forgive me, bro!"

Julius just glared at him. "Never."

"What?" Brutus asked with disbelief.

"I'm never gonna forgive you," Julius scolded coldly as he turned around and laid back down, beginning to softly sob again. "Now get out of my room." All Brutus could do was leave his room quietly, close the door, sit down on the floor and bury his face in his hands.

* * *

"Brutus?"

He slowly opened his eyes and looked up at me. After he threw up on my bed and passed out, I managed to drag his large body to the bathtub to clean him up. I planned on going back to sleep, but I had to stay up to make sure he didn't drown himself.

"I'm glad you woke up alright," I said to him with a soft smile.

Brutus looked around and lifted his arms out of the water. "How did I get here?"

"You threw up on me and my bed and I cleaned you up."

"You pulled me to this bathtub all by yourself?" he asked with a raised eyebrow.

"Yes. I don't know how, but I did it. Just goes to show how much I care."

He looked away with a sharp nod of the head. "Uh-uh, sis. I'm a bad person. You shouldn't waste your time on me."

"...where did that come from?"

Brutus looked down for a moment and nervously licked his lip. "Remember Uncle Posei?"

"Yeah. Whatever happened to him?"

"Mama told him to stop coming around us."

"Why?"

"On Christmas back in '85, me and Julius were playing the new Atari that Dad got us. We was in the middle of a game of *Asteroids*, when he just walked into Julius's room, unannounced."

"What happened?"

"He told us to stop playing the game and stood in front of us, saying he wanted to play Eeny, Meanie, Miny, Moe. When he got to the last moe, his finger landed on Julius." Brutus paused to rub his shoulder and wince. "He grabbed Julius and told me to stay where I was and watch. He made Julius sit on the bed and pulled his pants down. He... he did *things* to him."

My skin cooled as I let out a strong gasp. I was utterly mortified. "Just when I thought our family's secrets couldn't get any darker."

* * *

Pan sat on the edge of the bed as the golden crack of dawn peered through the blinds of the window in the motel room. He looked at the clock and let out a smirk when he saw that it was 5:45 A.M. He lit up and began puffing on a cigar, as his mistress crawled up to him and gently groped him around the neck.

"One more round?" Theia whispered.

Pan gently removed her arm from around his neck before answering seductively. "You know I'd love to, but today's not the day."

Theia rolled over on the bed with a raised eyebrow. "Well, you're more post-coital than usual this morning."

Pan took another puff of his cigar as he looked back at her. "You know, over the past year I've been seeing you at this motel, not even a drop of guilt comes to my brow whenever I lay in bed with my wife the morning after." Pan laughed. "Who would have ever thought I'd feel guilty once I knew the favor was being returned?"

Theia stared at him. "What are you getting at?"

Pan just let out a devious smirk. "Payback is a motherfucker."

Theia brushed back her hair, staring Pan coldly in the eye. "Your wife is having an affair of her own?"

"I don't know for a fact," Pan replied between cigar puffs. "But all the signs are there."

Theia rolled her eyes and laid across him. "You fucking hypocrite."

"If I'm a burnt pot, you're nothing more than a scorched kettle."

Theia chuckled. "Say you ever meet her paramour, yes? What would you do to him?

Pan paused before taking another hit of his cigar to glare at Theia. "Why on Earth would you ask me that?"

"Because I know exactly what Odysseus would do to you," she said, caresing his chest, and poking his nose. "He'd more than likely kill you."

* * *

Brutus and I stood on the balcony of our parent's room, looking at the house next door. It was previously unoccupied, but someone was moving in that day. We continued to talk, observing the movers hard at work.

"So because of what happened with Uncle Posei, you don't think Julius won't forgive you?"

Brutus nodded. "He told me himself he would never forgive

me for that night. And for years, the two of us just... didn't talk about it. I figure if he never forgave me for that, he ain't gonna forgive me for getting him disowned."

"Brutus, he didn't understand back then. Even though he was the one being touched, Uncle Posei still *made* you sit there and watch. He had control over both of you and you were just a boy. There wasn't anything you could have done."

"You still don't get it! It was like the start of a domino effect. Ever since, I've only done wrong by him. If he never wanted to see or talk to me again, I'd understand."

I shook my head. "Bro, I wasn't that little when some of this stuff happened. Remember when you wrote the phone number in the girl's bathroom and framed him for it? I'm sure he's let that go by now. As for getting him disowned and what happened with Uncle Posei, I'm sure if you just talk to him, he'll understand."

Brutus was still fixated on the house next door, clearly trying to run away from the conversation. "Man, this lady moving in sure is uppity!"

I rolled my eyes and turned to look back at the house. I saw the pieces of furniture entering the house and immediately saw where he was coming from. Between the shiny, white baby grand piano adorned with gilt, the Monet and Rembrandt paintings, the Hellenistic-style sculptures of well-muscled, barely clothed men and women and the white Jaguar Vanden Plas in the driveway, I could tell our new neighbor was someone who had a taste for nothing but the finest things in life.

Looking closer at the porte-cochere, I gulped and felt a slight chill when I saw Magister Hadrian standing there. Dressed in a brown, velvet suit that had to cost at least a grand, he was talking to a short, rounded woman in a bright amber pantsuit with big, brown hair in a style akin to Farrah Fawcett.

After a couple of moments, Magister Hadrian pointed towards us. The lady turned around for us to see her face. She had pasty skin with profound, naturally rosy cheeks, and deep blue eyes. She closed in on me, scowling her eyes into one of the most powerfully frightening glares I had ever seen. Her piercing gaze was so profound and full of hatred, I began to feel sick.

Brutus, shrugged his shoulders. "Man, what they lookin' at us like that for?"

"I don't know," I said with shortness of breath as I started to lose my balance. "I'm starting to feel kinda dizzy,"

"Yo Cali, you alright?"

"I... I... don't... think so."

* * *

Demeter was all smiles as she wrote the weekly specials on the chalkboard. With the school year starting the following week, and having made more than enough revenue, she decided to finally outsource employment outside of her family. Her first new hire walked in as she continued to decorate the chalkboard.

"Good morning Troy," Demeter said cheerily.

Troy nodded. "Good morning."

Demeter reached over to shake his hand and smiled as she gave him a tour of The Cornucopia. She enthused over everything while he responded with a silent nod here and a slight chuckle there. As she explained his daily tasks, Cicero confidently sauntered into the door with Versace sunglasses, a big smile and a lit cigar in hand.

"Good morning beautiful!" Cicero yelled in an enthusiastic, saucy manner.

"Good morning to you too. Um, Troy, this is Cicero. He's a businessman in the area who always assists me with running The Cornucopia. Cicero, Troy. Excuse us for a moment," Demeter said nervously, motioning for Cicero to follow her to the back office. As they walked inside, Cicero quickly shut the door behind them and pulled her in for a kiss. After a flirty embrace, Demeter broke the kiss and shoved him away softly. "Now, now, Cicero, you don't want the whole town to know about us, do you?"

Cicero laughed as he eyed her up and down seductively. "Everybody already knows I hate my wife. And there's no doubt in your mind that Pan's cheating. Why don't we just break things off with them already?!"

Cicero caressed her back and rested his large head on her shoulder. "I know I'm not happy, but I can't get a divorce! I'm a Christian woman!"

"Is that so? You must have forgotten about that the first night you gave it up in this office."

Demeter moved her shoulder away, but didn't break his embrace. "I'm still praying about that sin every night." She placed her head on his chest and sighed heavily, breathing in his scent. "Oh, who am I kidding? Pan and I are both going to hell! And these affairs won't be the only reason."

Cicero stroked her chin. "So how about having some more fun while you still can?"

Demeter looked up at him with a smile on her face as he growled like a wolf. They began to kiss passionately. Demeter rubbed his back up and down as Cicero firmly gripped her derriere. Cicero reached underneath her dress as she began to unbutton his shirt, readying another encounter, but they were interrupted by a knock at the door.

They backed away from each other quickly and Demeter fixed her slightly askew dress. "Who is it?"

"It's Troy," he said from the other side of the door. "I made cappuccinos for the two of you."

"Thank you Troy!" Demeter enthused as Cicero stood in a corner and wiped sweat off his brow. "We'll be out to get them in a minute! I know you did a good job."

"I completely forgot that kid was even here," Cicero said, taking another puff of his cigar.

Demeter side-eyed him. "Exactly! Be more discrete next time!" They left the office and saw Troy hard at work behind the counter with two neatly frothed cappuccinos sitting on the table.

Demeter took a sip and smiled. "Troy, you're a natural! Only your first day and everything about this cappuccino is just right." Cicero nodded in agreement.

"Thanks," Troy said with a chuckle as Cicero choked on his cigar. "My uncle Cleon runs a coffee shop in the Cascade, so I know a thing or two about making drinks."

Troy proceeded to continue wiping down the counter, baking pastries and running the coffee machines as Demeter cheerily looked on. Meanwhile, Cicero sat down, continuing to nurse his cappuccino with a look of suspended belief on his face. Troy paused momentarily, staring at Cicero knowingly.

"What are you looking at, kid?" Cicero asked with attitude.

"You look like someone I knew when I was a kid."

"I don't know what you're talking about," Cicero bit back before taking a hit of his cigar.

"Just a coincidence, I'm sure." Troy shrugged before he went back to work. "Don't worry about it, big man."

Demeter turned to him. "Is everything okay?"

Cicero motioned for her to come closer and whispered in her ear. "Did that kid just say he has an uncle named Cleon?"

"Yes, I believe so," Demeter whispered.

"And he runs a coffee shop in the Cascade?"

"Is that some sort of problem?"

Cicero took one last puff of his cigar. "I don't trust him."

Demeter grimaced. "Why?"

Cicero looked over to Troy and hushed his voice to a whisper. "My people have a history with the Lords of The Cascade. Cleon happens to be one of their leaders."

* * *

"Give me back my baby!"

"Who's that?" I asked softly, opening my eyes. Looking around, all I could see was a set of stairs leading to a faintly lit room at the peak before I felt around frantically in an attempt to figure out what was going on.

"How did I end up here?"

"Turn yourself in to Odysseus and we will!" I heard a familiar voice say.

"Is... is that Magister Hadrian?" I said aloud, making my way up the stairs.

At the staircase's peak, I laid my eyes upon the torture chamber, only this time, someone was tied to the wheel. It was the woman who had been coming to me in my dreams. Standing in front of her, with their backs to me, was Magister Hadrian with a short woman beside him.

"Never!" she pleaded. "I will not give in to The Acropolis!"

"Tsk, tsk, that will never do," the woman said, revealing her profile as turned to look at him. It was then that I realized who she was. She was the woman moving in next door.

"Did I just travel back in time?" I whispered, scratching my head. .

"You're right, that will never do," Hadrian seconded to the woman. "What say you, Narcissus?"

I gulped. Narcissus was the fascist councilwoman from the past so many had told me about. I was hoping I would never meet her and yet there she was, moving in right next door.

Narcissus let out a laugh so exaggerated and maniacal, it was almost demonic. "I suggest we pull out the dagger rack. Then, I'll have you spin the wheel while I try my luck. If she survives, we'll turn her in to Odysseus. If not, we're just going to have to bury her! Either way, her baby is the reward for our bounty hunters!"

Hadrian laughed. "You are just pure evil. I love it!"

The woman tied to the wheel screamed. "NO! YOU CAN'T DO THIS!"

"Oh yes we can!" Narcissus retorted, pulling out the rack of daggers she spoke of earlier.

"Even if you kill me, you will get yours one day! And so will Odysseus! One day, The Acropolis will fall!" The woman pleaded as Hadrian approached the wheel and motioned to start spinning.

"YOU GUYS CAN'T DO THIS!" I yelled, but no one appeared to hear me. I ran towards Hadrian, attempting to pry his arm away from the wheel but my hands went right through him as if he was a mass of air.

The woman cried as Narcissus glared at her deviously. "I'm ready to have a little fun. Aren't you?"

"YOU'LL BURN IN HELL FOR THIS, BITCH!"

"I'm going to hell? That's awfully rich coming from you!"

Narcissus scoffed as Hadrian started spinning the wheel. She picked up one of the daggers and threw it towards her.

I ran in front of the woman, reaching my arms out. "NO! STOP!"

"Cali, wake up!"

I sat up immediately and stretched my arms out. "NO! PLEASE DON'T KILL HER!"

"What?" Brutus asked, scratching his head.

I looked around to see that Brutus and I were in our parent's room. It was still daylight outside. My ears were ringing and my head throbbed.

"What just happened?" I asked.

"You just collapsed out of nowhere! You blacked out and hit your head on the wall pretty hard too."

I looked at Brutus, pulling my legs up towards my chest. "We're no longer safe in this house, Brutus."

"Why do you say that?"

I inhaled without fully comprehending what I was about to say: "Narcissus the witch-hunter has moved in next door and she won't rest until I'm made an untouchable."

IV

Awakening

Class Is In Session

I slowly pried my eyes open as sunlight broke in through my blinds. The final week of summer breezed by, and it was time to enter my worst nightmare: my first day at Pegasus High School. All I could feel inside was a heavy boulder of dread.

I hated the thought of walking through those halls, but I sucked my teeth and got out of bed anyway. I showered, brushed my teeth and played with my hair, before heading to Isis and Atum's rooms to check on them, but they had already gotten out of bed and made their way downstairs. I walked past Julius's old room and my heart dropped like a two-ton dumbbell. His absence caused everything to feel so off. I held back tears as I made my way to Brutus's room. Unsurprisingly, he was still fast asleep, snoring like a grizzly bear, with the faint scent of marijuana still lingering in his room.

"Okay, bro, I don't wanna go and I know you don't either, but it's time to wake up," I said, patting him on the back, only for him to reply with a loud, pungent fart. With his eyes still closed, he let out a sigh of relief and rubbed his belly.

"Ugh, really Brutus?" I complained, holding my hand over my nose.

"Better out than in, sis," he laughed, slowly beginning to open his eyes.

I made my way to the bathroom as he got out of bed, passing more flatulence along the way. I brushed my teeth, washed my face, and quickly hopped in the shower. After drying myself off and putting on my clothes, I stood in front of the mirror, trying to force a smile in an attempt to cheer myself up, but it was no use. I didn't feel optimistic about anything. All I could do was sigh as I looked somberly upon my reflection.

I heard a knock on the bathroom door. "Just a minute."

"Yo sis, I don't think I can wait another a minute!" Brutus laughed. "Those farts are turning into somethin' else!"

I cringed. "Alright, go ahead and take care of your business." I opened the door, and Brutus practically ran me over as I walked out.

I could smell breakfast being cooked downstairs, but didn't feel the slightest bit hungry. Going back to my room, I turned on the radio just as the DJ introduced "One Last Cry" by Brian McKnight. I laid on the bed, alone in my thoughts and played with my hair.

"What a day. And it hasn't even begun yet." I got back out of bed, put on my clothes, picked up my tote bag and made my way downstairs. I entered the kitchen, and for the first time in months, I saw Mama preparing one of her famous breakfasts and humming away in front of the stove.

"Good morning, Calliope!" she shouted happily with a big smile.

"Good morning to you too," I said in a tone that couldn't have been anymore deadpan while I stared at her. I couldn't help but to wonder what had gotten into her after the weeks of negativity. Isis and Atum quickly bolted past me and smashed into her.

"Good morning babies!" she exclaimed, reciprocating their hugs.

"Mama, is everything okay?" I asked, raising my eyebrows.

She laughed. "Therapy is a beautiful thing. I've been feeling much better lately."

I stared at her while I silently shook my head and made myself a plate of bacon, eggs and sugared grits before taking a seat at the table and starting to eat. While Isis and Atum were talking to Mama, they all turned to the kitchen doorway. Their smiles immediately reversed when they saw Brutus standing there, with a snide half-smile on his face.

"Damn family, I knew I wasn't popular, but can a brotha get a good morning?"

"Good morning Brutus," I said cheerily before side-eyeing Mama.

He rubbed his belly and nodded his head. "Good to see someone's showin' me love." He made himself a plate of food and we all sat at the table, eating in silence when Dad walked in.

He stood at the kitchen counter, pouring himself a glass of orange juice like it wasn't the first time any of us had seen him in days. We turned to look at him as he gulped down the glass of juice. He let out a sigh of refreshment before he looked at us and realized we had been staring at him. "Is it my face?"

Mama nodded her head. "No, it's her perfume all over your clothes."

Brutus put his hand over face. "Aww shit, Mama! You actually went there!"

"Please, can we not this morning?" I chimed in.

"You're absolutely right, Calliope," Mama agreed. "We shouldn't this morning. Not. At. All." She got out of her seat and threw her plate in the sink as she looked him up and down. She looked as if she was about to say something, but instead she just shook her head and stormed out of the kitchen.

Dad shrugged. "What was all of that about?"

"I'm pretty sure you know," Atum answered smartly.

"Don't speak to me with that tone, boy!"

I just shook my head. "Why are you so mad? It's not like you deserve any respect from us."

"Excuse me!?" he exclaimed, raising his eyebrow.

"Ay Cali, don't go there!" Brutus cautioned.

"No, I think we need to have this conversation," I said sternly, getting out of my seat and walking over to him. "Why should we respect you? We don't see you for days, only for you to come home drenched in Chanel No. 5. You move us all away from the only home we've ever known. You've made us affiliates of the Griffin Mafia against our will. You put Brutus in harm's way by having him do god knows what for Romulus and Cicero at that nightclub down the road. You ruined Julius's life because you didn't want him to be happy. You're not a good father, you're not a good husband, and you're not a good person."

My siblings were all stunned in shock and I couldn't help but to let out a little smile once I finished my speech. I held back a chuckle as I saw him clench his teeth and his eyes fumed like molten lava.

"I put a roof over your head, food in your stomach and clothes on your back and you have the nerve to speak to me like that, you ungrateful little cretin!?"

"I just did, didn't I?"

"Is that right? I have the power to disown you, young lady! Remember that!"

I tossed my plate in the sink with a laugh. "You sure about that? Word on the street is, you ain't my real dad anyway." I gave Isis and Atum kisses on their foreheads and made my way out the front door. "I'll meet you outside, bro," I said to Brutus, who stood there speechless.

* * *

"Is she ever gonna reply?" Julius said to himself as he laid in the bed, quietly staring at the ceiling with his nerves in an anxious tingle. "I wonder if Brutus wants to talk."

Pothos walked in the front door. "Honey, I'm home!"

Julius couldn't help but to smirk as Pothos made his way to the bedroom and hopped on the bed, handing over the mail. Julius bolted through the mail to see if Calliope's letter was in there. He grimaced and laid back down to stare at the ceiling when he saw that it wasn't there once again.

Pothos' smile and bright eyes waned away into confusion and he rubbed Julius on the shoulder. "You okay, baby?"

"No, I'm not okay. It's been almost two weeks since I sent that letter to Calliope and she hasn't gotten back to me yet!"

Pothos shook his head. "I'm sure she's been going through a lot right now. Just give her some time."

"What if she never even saw the letter to begin with? For all we know, Pan saw it and threw it away."

"Now, now, this is no time to be dramatic," Pothos assured. "Besides, you didn't even notice you got a letter from that diner in the Cascade."

Julius sat back up with his eyes widened in surprise. He sifted through the mail again until he saw the letter and opened it quickly.

Dear Julius,

This is Eros from the Hecate Diner. I was very impressed with your interview for the cook position and decided that you are the best candidate for the job. Come on down this Thursday in black

pants, black shoes and a white shirt.
  Congrats,
  Eros

* * *

"Here we are," Brutus said nonchalantly as we stood across the street from Pegasus High. At three stories tall, it brought to mind a foreboding, ancient Roman temple. Six imposing pillars ran from the flat, red-tiled roof through each story of the building to the ground, with two slightly faded bronze emblems of a winged horse flanking the row of pillars on each side. Each of the large, gilded windows felt as if they were staring down at us with contempt.

"I'm not gonna lie," I said with a gulp. "I'm nervous."

Brutus turned to me and laughed. "Well you ain't never been to school before." I could tell he was trying to chill me out, but the tremble in his voice and his uneasy eyes told me he knew that wasn't what I meant.

We both stared at the school across the street, when I noticed the girl who lived next door walking up the school's steps. She paused to turn around and looked in our direction. I looked at Brutus, noticing that he was eyeing her as well.

"Oooh, Brutus, who's that?" I said flirtatiously.

He scoffed. "That ain't nobody."

"Is that your little girl-toy?" I laughed. "I remember that night you were walking outside the house half-naked.

"Let's just get this done and over with," he said nervously, making his way across the street and into the school. I let him walk a few steps in front of me before I followed suit. I didn't expect to tail him all around school every day.

Brutus walked into the school, while I found refuge under an oak tree until the bell rung. I noticed the jocks and cheerleaders flirting with one another on the front steps.

"Is there anything you like to do besides football?" I heard one of the cheerleaders ask cynically.

"Uh, not really. But I'm way cooler than these nerds over here playing *Magic: The Gathering!*" a jock teased towards two boys with glasses, flannel shirts and messy hair playing the game at a table next to the steps. The entire crowd burst out in laughter as they reddened with embarrassment. I couldn't do anything but shake my head at the sight.

"BOO!" I heard a girl exclaim behind me. My heart leaped for a second before I noticed it was Fortuna.

"Fortuna!" I exclaimed warmly, giving her a hug.

"Prepared for your first day in hell?"

I laughed. "Not really, but I'm sure I'll survive."

"Well, good luck. You're gonna need it," she responded, rolling her eyes.

I looked back at the table, shaking my head as the jocks continued to mock the two boys playing their card game. "I guess I shouldn't play *Magic* at school unless I want to get made fun of."

Fortuna chuckled a bit. "It doesn't matter. Card games or not, the cheerleaders and the jocks will find some reason to talk shit about you. It's best just to ignore them. The cheerleaders are a pack of annoying bitches and the jocks all need to have their faces bashed in, but they're all pretty harmless for the most part. If there's anyone to watch out for, it's the M.I.T and the trust fund girls. They will really screw you over if you cross them."

"M.I.T.? What's that?"

"Mobsters in Training. If anyone knows about them, it's me.

Now, the Trusties on the other hand? You already got a taste of their tyranny when you met Eriserable and Moirtem."

I felt uneasy as the bell rung. Walking into the school with Fortuna, I couldn't help but gulp at the thought that there was a pack of girls who were just like the two of them.

* * *

"Ah... ah... ah... oh... oh my... OH MY GOD!" Medea yelled in the third floor girl's bathroom of Pegasus High while Brutus's face was between her legs. "OH MY GOD! BRUTUS I LOVE YOU!"

Brutus paused before he covered her mouth. "Girl hush! You tryin' to get both of us expelled?!"

Medea forcefully removed his hand. "Relax, you brute. We're not going to get caught. Everyone has fucked in this bathroom at least once."

Brutus's eyes grew wide as he looked at the floor and promptly jumped to his feet. "Why didn't you tell me there was caked-on cum all over the floor?" He unlocked the stall door and made his way to the sink to wash his hands.

Medea pulled up her pants and walked over to the sink. "You know I don't really love you, right?"

"I don't love you either. You're just fun to fuck." Brutus finished washing his hands and reached for a paper towel. "How come it's so easy for people to hook up in this bathroom?"

Medea laughed. "The third floor has been unused since the early '80s. You can get away with murder up here."

"Is that so?" Brutus replied with a raised eyebrow.

"Everyone thinks the third floor is haunted, so if anyone hears a scream, they'll just think it's a ghost," she explained as a football player and cheerleader kissed before locking themselves in one of the stalls.

"I see," Brutus said, looking at the closed stall door. "What exactly went down up here for the school to shut it down?"

Medea shirked from her cool demeanor as her eyes twitched and her voice trembled. "Let's just say it's something people in Griffin don't like to talk about."

***

As I and the other students crowded in the ornate, golden gymnasium for the principal's first day speech, I pretty much clinged onto Fortuna as we gazed around at everyone with mousiness. Hardly any of the faces were familiar to me. I couldn't help but wonder where everyone had come from.

Fortuna looked to me with a laugh. "The reason you don't recognize anyone is because over half the kids leave during the summer months. Just about everyone's parents here has a yacht in Savannah Beach or a condo on the island." I noticed Moirai and another girl wearing the same demeanor, presumably one of the Trusties, walking up to find a seat in the bleachers.

They both eyed me before Moirai turned to her friend and pointed at me. "Watch out for that one," she said, giving me the evil eye.

"You see that girl walking with Moirai?" Fortuna whispered in my ear. "That's Atropos. You *really* need to watch out for her. She's the principal's niece and can have you expelled in a second. Speaking of which, here comes the fat bastard himself." she said as we looked at the podium on the gym floor.

Mr. Erebus was a short, portly man with a reddened face and beady, green eyes behind square-framed glasses. His receding hairline gave way to wispy, upstanding hairs on the midshaft of his head, giving him the appearance of a mad scientist. He wore navy blue pants, a navy blue blazer and a light blue shirt that looked as if he might burst out of it at any second.

Before beginning his speech, he performed one of the most exaggerated inhales I had ever seen. "It is here today that I welcome you all to the beginning of a new year at Pegasus High," he said with a voice as ornery as he looked.

"Sounds like a lot of fun, doesn't it?" Fortuna scoffed as I nodded.

"It is a pleasure to not only welcome back returning students but to also see all of our new faces." He took a pause to look around before continuing nervously. "I see that we've grown progressively more... ahem... *diverse* this year."

"Oh yeah, we could all use a little more chocolate in our lives!" a random girl yelled from somewhere in the gymnasium, followed by a combination of laughter and jeers.

"Now, now, behave yourselves!" Mr. Erebus yelled. "I understand a lot of you aren't used to a multicultural environment, but times are changing and there's nothing we can do about it. I guess we will all have to learn to be more sensitive."

Fortuna elbowed me cynically. "Way to show your support, Principal Erebus."

"Recently, I've been alerted by Magister Hadrian of some growing concerns in the community. In addition to our steadily changing ethnic demographic, it's been speculated that witches and other people with powers have been moving in discretely. I am not going to make any hasty assumptions, of course, but this will be the first and only warning: anyone who is caught in the act or under reasonable suspicion of taking part in supernatural actions will be immediately expelled, arrested and taken to Griffin Council Hall to await trial!"

"I am sure you all are aware of just how devastating the Ruptures have been to our fair city-state in the past. In order to prevent another from happening, I'm afraid this is a necessary precaution. By all means, I would like for those of you who don't take part in such evil to assist in the process. Refrain from hastily pointing fingers, but if you have any suspicions, be sure to let a member of our faculty know immediately."

"I'll be sure to arrive first thing in the morning with a pitchfork!" one of the jocks yelled out as the others laughed raucously.

"They should know better anyway, especially after that whole mess with the Crimson Maiden," I heard a girl say from the row behind us.

Shivers crawled up my spine as everyone in the auditorium let out a series of jeers after the principal's speech. I couldn't help but feel like everyone was looking at me. The Oracle was right. Another rupture was brewing.

Pegasus High Society 101

After the assembly was over, Fortuna and I walked to the cafeteria to pick up our schedules. Since she was a junior, she had to wait in a different line, so we made some more chit chat before parting ways. As I waited in line, it still felt like everyone's eyes were on me. What Principal Erebus said about witches had me completely shook. I was so unnerved by it, I tuned out the rest of his speech, playing the words again and again in my head.

"Name?" the older woman at the desk asked.

I was so caught up in my paranoia I didn't realized it was my turn in line. "Calliope. Calliope Thessaly."

The woman looked through the folder on her desk and handed me my schedule. I thanked her and went on my way, taking a look at my schedule.

Period I: Sophomore English & Literature with Mrs. Loukas

Period II: Biology with Mr. Chiklis

Period III: Sophomore Art with Mrs. Corinth

Period IV: Geometry with Mr. Ambrosius

Period V: World History with Ms. Alexandros

Period VI: Sophomore Physical Education with Mrs. Catranide

The room for Sophomore English & Literature was on the second floor, so I made my way up the stairs. I had never felt more shy and awkward, practically sticking to the wall next to the staircase, trying to make myself as invisible as possible. But much to my chagrin, since my skin, my hair and my clothes were different than everyone else around, I couldn't help but draw a few stares.

As I reached the top of the staircase and eyed the room for my class, I saw Eris, Moirai and Atropos, making chit chat in front of the door. I ducked behind one of the lockers and observed, waiting for them to disperse. A few seconds later, they burst out into laughter. Moirai and Atropos went about their way, while Eris made her way into the classroom.

As I approached the classroom, I heard Eris yell out "Hey mom!" I gulped and walked up to the door, timidly peering in, only to see Eris and Hestia talking to each other. I walked in quietly and took a seat in the back of the classroom, hoping no one would notice. The bell rung and several other students rushed in as Eris took her seat in the very front row.

"Good morning class!" Hestia began. "Welcome to Sophomore English & Literature! I assume everyone here had a good summer vacation?"

Everyone around me mumbled a variety of things, while I sat low in my seat, trying to pretend I didn't exist. She began the student roll call, never shirking from her bubbly demeanor. When she called her daughter's name, she said it with a sickeningly sweet tone. The smile on her face beamed bright as her daughter said "present" with the perfect amount of ditz and I groaned at the obvious favoritism. Once she got to my name, the enthusiasm vanished and she stared at the paper with disdain. "Calliope Thessaly?"

I sat up a little in my seat and gulped. "Here."

I could feel everyone's eyes as they turned to me, sitting

timidly in my seat. Hestia was both bemused and disgruntled when she saw me.

"Pleasure to have you in my class, Calliope," she said cynically, placing her roll call sheet back on her desk. "Do you know one thing I don't appreciate from my students?"

"What would that be?" I asked timidly.

"Docility. And of all the students here, you had the weakest response of everyone when your name was called. Because of that, I would prefer that you took this open seat in the front, next to my daughter Eris, instead of sitting in the back."

"Yes, ma'am," I said nervously, moving to my new seat. Eris shot me a glare as I sat down next to her while Hestia began to lecture. I sank down timidly in my chair, trying in vain to make myself invisible.

* * *

Fortuna took a seat at the back of her U.S. History class, nonchalantly popping gum and refusing to pay a lick of attention to a word the teacher was saying. She was focused on the clock to see how much longer until class was over, when she caught wind of someone staring at her. She looked to the front of the class, to see Atropos and another Trustie snickering at her. She rolled her eyes and shook her head, looking back at the clock when she felt a wad of paper hit her in the head.

What the fuck? Fortuna thought to herself as she picked up the piece of paper and unfolded it.

Dear UnFortuna,

Stop popping that gum! You look like a cow munching on grass! You're interrupting our learning experience! Very unladylike!

Fortuna clenched her teeth and groaned before rolling the

piece of paper back up into a wad and throwing it at Atropos, who let out a yelp and raised her hand.

"Ms. Alexandros!" Atropos blurted out, interrupting the lecture. "Fortuna just threw a piece of a paper at me!"

"Not even a day into the school year and you're already causing trouble, Fortuna?"

"Atropos threw it at me first! And she said I look like a cow!"

"*Doesn't she ever get tired of being an angry loser?*" Fortuna heard the student next to her say.

She turned to the student to retort. "Oh shut up!"

He looked at Fortuna with confusion, shrugging his shoulders. "I didn't say anything."

"My, my, Fortuna, you're being awfully disruptive!" Ms. Alexandros exclaimed as Fortuna stared at her wide-eyed. "Perhaps you need to take a seat at the front of the class."

"Yes, ma'am," Fortuna sighed, making her way up the aisle while everyone stared at her. Also in the front row, she saw Atropos and her friend staring mockingly before snickering at her. As Fortuna took her seat, she folded her arms and smacked her lips at them.

* * *

Brutus stepped into the cafeteria, looking around for Calliope. He saw a number of cliques that he wasn't used to, coming from Campe High in Auburn. At one table, he saw kids with their hair in spikes, bright colors and unusual cuts. At another, he saw two kids in berets painting and drinking coffee. Towards the front, he saw a group of girls, half wearing 1950s style dresses and the others dressed like spreads from *Cosmopolitan* or *Vogue*. They were talking to a group of boys in designer suits and sunglasses, looking directly out of a Mafia film. When he saw there was no sign of Calliope, Brutus groaned and took a seat at a table by himself.

"These kids around here are on some weird ass shit," Brutus noted as he saw a large man approaching him. With a short hi-top fade haircut, big lips and a very large body dressed in a football jersey, he shot a head nod as he neared Brutus's table.

"About time I see another brotha around here!"

The guy laughed. "What's up? You're Brutus, right?"

"You've heard about me already, huh?"

"Just a little bit," the guy said, taking a seat next to Brutus and offering him a handshake. "Name's Momus."

"Since we're the two token black guys 'round here, I guess you wanna be friends?"

"There's a few of us around here, man. Most of them just hang out with the other cliques."

"They wanna be like these weirdos around here, huh? Man, these kids would be clowned all day if we were in Auburn."

"Yeah," Momus laughed, before his face twisted into a frown. "So, um, the reason why I'm over here talkin' to you is cuz I heard about you and Medea."

Brutus's eyes grew wide and he broke into a cold sweat. "What'd you hear, exactly?"

"Just that y'all been hooking up lately," Momus replied matter-of-factly.

"Okay... *and*?!" Brutus asked in an argumentative tone. "Why do you care?"

"She's my ex," Momus whispered uneasily, glancing around the cafeteria.

Brutus started fuming. "Let me get this straight, you mad I'm fuckin' Medea because she used to be your girl? Don't be actin' all jealous just cuz you blew your chance!"

Brutus pounded on his chest as several students at nearby tables turned to look at them. Momus shook his head and shushed him.

"I ain't jealous of a damn thang! I'm tryin' to look out for you! That girl ain't any good. Step out of line with her once and she'll throw you under the bus in a second!"

"And why I should trust you?"

Momus smacked his lips. "Used to be a star football player at this school, man. Penn State lined me up with a full ride and it was only my junior year. Too bad I was in love with Medea though. I broke up with her when I realized all she cared about was my dick and pissing off her dad. Then she ran and told those boys in the Armani suits all about it." He chuckled. "They tried to whoop my ass, but I got that situation handled real quick. The principal didn't like it though. Got kicked off the football team and had my scholarship taken away from me the week after. All because of her."

Brutus paused for a moment, before rolling his eyes. "Man, pussy is pussy to me! I ain't tryin' to go to college!"

"You think that matters? Trust me, she will find some way to ruin your life if you keep hooking up with her! Mark my words!"

"I ain't even tryin' to hear that shit," Brutus said, getting up from his seat. "I think I'll take my lunch break outside. Griffin already wack enough as it is without house niggas like you tryin' to warn me about nothing."

A Night At The Megalopolis

At the end of the day, I saw Brutus waiting at the bottom of the school steps and couldn't help but to smash into him. I had never been so relieved to see him.

"Damn, sis!" he exclaimed in confusion. "It's only been six hours."

"Bro, I just had one of the worst days of my life in there."

Brutus chuckled. "Alright, tell me all about it."

We started to walk home as I told him all about being class-mates with Eris in a class where her mother was also the teacher and mentioned Moirai, Atropos and the other Trusties eyeing me all day. I told him I hated being stared at by so many other students like I was some sort of freak.

"And to top it all off, I didn't see you or Fortuna all day! I felt so alone, I was just so happy to see you when it was all over!" I finished.

"You know, I never thought I'd see the day where'd you be happy to see me," Brutus said with a smirk on his face.

"Me either, but here we are."

"You may not believe it, but that makes me really happy," he said as we reached Ponos Street. "Perseus is coming through, we're gonna have a little smoke session. You down to join?"

I paused and pondered the question, before I gave a shrug.

"Sure." A red Jeep pulled up, blasting "Steady Mobbin'" by Ice Cube. Perseus was with his friend Karm in the passenger seat. He was a short man of dark complexion with a bald head and stout build.

"Big B!" Perseus yelled, rolling down the windows, reaching out to Brutus for a handshake.

"Perseus! My man!" Brutus shouted back as he approached his car and shook his hand. He acknowledged Karm as well and they exchanged a few words before Brutus pointed at me.

"Hey, just so you know, Cali wants to join in on the fun."

Perseus turned to look at me, perplexed. "You invited her? I thought you didn't like her like that?"

"Nah man, she's cool," Brutus scoffed as he opened the door to the backseat, motioning for me to join. I greeted Perseus who gave me a nod and joined Brutus in the backseat.

Numerous rap songs blared over the speakers as Brutus and Perseus talked the whole way with Karm adding a few words here and there. I sat quietly, taking in the scenery. After about ten minutes, we reached a two-story villa on the outskirts of the city, isolated in the woods. It was multicolored, utilizing shades of purple, red, gold and blue in the décor with fanciful arches and statuary adorning the porte cochere. The statues were in a number of suggestive positions and seemed to glare at us with contempt, as they surrounded a doorway that led into a dark void.

A thick, dark air permeated the estate. As I glanced upon the building, I did not sense any welcoming energy. It was something sinister and oppressive. Just the air alone, agitated my soul.

I turned to Brutus who was staring at the place nervously. "Is this The Megalopolis?"

Perseus and Karm made their way out of the car, while Brutus and I looked upon the place with chills, permeating through our spines. I was too spooked to even move.

"Yo, is y'all coming or what!?" Perseus yelled. Brutus got out of the car hesitantly, with me following behind.

I plodded towards the entrance, as Brutus tailed Perseus and Karm. As we approached the door, Brutus turned to look at me, and gave me a nod as he walked in.

I was so frightened by the place I couldn't even move. On one of the columns in the entryway, there was a fanciful sign, detailing the rules.

SIR PHILOPOEMEN

WELCOMES YOU TO

THE MEGALOPOLIS

HERE BE A PAVILLON OF HEDONISTIC PLEASURE. A NIGHT HERE IS A NIGHT I PROMISE THAT YOU'LL NEVER REMEMBER TO FORGET.

ALL ARE WELCOME, AS LONG AS THEY ABIDE BY THESE SIMPLE RULES

*I. INEBRIATION OF SOME SORT IS AN ABSOLUTE REQUIREMENT IN **THE MEGALOPOLIS**, UNLESS YOU HAVE BEEN GRANTED PER-MISSION TO ENJOY THIS PALACE IN AUSTERITY*

*II. ONE IS TO NEVER SPEAK OF WHAT TOOK PLACE WITHIN THE WALLS OF **THE MEGALOPOLIS***

*III. ONE IS NEVER TO CAPTURE, WHETHER IN PHOTOGRAPH OR REPORT, WHAT TOOK PLACE WITHIN THE WALLS OF **THE MEGALOPOLIS***

*IV. THIS IS A SANCTIONED MEETING PLACE FOR THE ATALAN UNDERWORLD, THOSE OUTSIDE OF THAT REALM ARE NOT TO MEDDLE IN THEIR AFFAIRS WITHIN **THE MEGALOPOLIS***

V. ANYONE WHO DARES SPEAK ILL OF THOSE WITH UPPER

NOBLE, ROYAL OR DIVINE STANDING WITHIN THE WALLS OF **THE MEGALOPOLIS** *WILL BE ESCORTED OUT AND PUNISHED*

OBSERVE THESE ORDERS, AND YOU CAN BE MERRY TO YOUR HEART'S CONTENT!

THE MEGALOPOLIS *AWAITS YOU!*

Although the bookends were welcoming, the board made the place feel even more foreboding. It was clear as ever why Julius and Brutus both were so shaken by the mere mention of the place. I looked back towards the eastern white pine trees of the forest surrounding the place, all swaying away in unison with the gentle breeze. It appeared that even the trees were afraid of the place. I shivered before I sighed and nervously made my way in.

* * *

Fortuna laid down underneath a Spanish moss tree in Pompeii Square, lit cigarette in one hand, Walkman in the other; her tape of choice being "Connected" by Stereo MCs. She took one hit after another, bopping her head to the music with her eyes closed.

"If you make sure you're connected, to the writings on the wall," she sang in a hushed voice as Pietas leaned over her.

"Singing to yourself again?" he laughed in a deadpan tone.

"Ugh, Pietas," she said, giving him a light punch on the arm. "You almost gave me a heart attack."

He laughed. "Isn't that the point?"

"Sure, if you want your girlfriend to go into cardiac arrest."

They both laid in the grass and talked while looking up at the dusk sky, ranting away about day one.

"Sometimes, I wish I could just shoot down that stupid winged horse," Fortuna scoffed. "I hate that place so much."

"Tell me about it," Pietas agreed, causing Fortuna to raise an eyebrow.

"You just started hanging out with M.I.T. though?"

"Whoa, whoa, how would you know that? We have different lunch periods!"

"So it's true then!" Fortuna exclaimed. "How could you start associating with them? You know I don't want them anywhere near me!"

Pietas shrugged. "They're cool people. They invited me to hang out with them at lunch and I did. What's the big deal?"

Fortuna's eyes sunk in and her face turned a little pale. "I don't trust them."

"Isn't your family part of the Mafia?"

"That's exactly why you can't trust them!" Fortuna shouted, gathering her stuff and walking away.

* * *

I sat quietly on one of the couches in the Megalopolis while Brutus talked to Perseus and Karm as they rolled blunts at the bar. Even though they were only a few feet away from me, I couldn't hear what they were saying. There was music playing in the background, but I couldn't hear it either. The dense, dark energy of the place drowned out any possible sound.

With imposing columns scattered throughout and velvet curtains in shades of red and purple framing the suites on the fringes of the room, the space was impressive. There was a small elevated stage and DJ podium in one of the corners with the bar in the center. Both were decorated in crystal-encrusted cream marble with a sparkle so dazzling, it was blinding. There was a sparkling disco ball and orange and red fluorescent lights illuminating the room.

And still, the space frightened me. It felt festive and welcoming, but I was terrified. I could feel something very dark and demonic lurking within the walls. All I could do was sit still while I watched Brutus, Perseus and Karm pass a blunt among themselves as I attempted to put my mind at ease.

"Now the party's about to get started!" Perseus shouted, looking towards the foyer.

I looked towards the foyer to see a short, stout man with a beard walk in, wearing a bright red suit and polished, dark-red gator skin monks, with three, statuesque women following suit. He had a dark complexion, and a deep, husky voice with several gold-plated teeth. He wielded a shiny, mahogany wood cane with a gold, diamond-encrusted head of a bull in one hand and a pungent cigar in the other. He looked like a pimp straight out of *Superfly* or *The Mack.* I couldn't help, but be a little charmed.

Perseus walked towards him and reached out for a handshake. "My man, Priapus!"

He nodded his head and returned the handshake. "Great to see you, Perseus! Been a while man!"

Karm joined in while Perseus and Priapus laughed and boasted about a variety of things as the three girls stood quietly behind him. My eyes turned to Brutus, who was still standing at the bar, practically drooling on himself at the sight of them.

"Oh, where are my manners?" Priapus boasted. "Let me introduce y'all to my lovely ladies over here. This right here is my newest arrival, Ariadne."

Ariadne smiled and stepped forward, slowly spinning in place. She was a tall, slender, busty woman with a haircut like Halle Berry. She had an hourglass shape, complemented by a skinny black dress she wore and long legs that were graceful like a flamingo. "Pleasure to meet you," she said flirtatiously in a soft, sultry voice, stroking Perseus's neck. He let out a quick hiccup as his eyes remained fixated on her.

Priapus laughed. "This right here is Phaedra."

Phaedra stepped under one of the spotlights and started to do a belly dance. She was more voluptuous than Ariadne in a brown, sleeveless catsuit. She had a diamond shaped face with skin like cinnamon, which belied dark, intimidating eyes. Her shoulder-length bobbed hair lightly bounced as she danced, pausing when she spotted Karm. She strutted over to him and rubbed his head, giving him a soft smirk.

"And don't let me forget my prized jewel, Pandora."

The room felt more silent than ever as we turned to look at her. She was the most intimidating of all as she was the tallest, the curviest, and commanded the most attention of the three, in spite of how quiet and still she remained. Her skin and eyes were both a light olive and her jet-black hair was sleek, smooth and straight. A mid-riff tank top bared her pierced navel as ripped acid-washed jeans and three-inch pumps completed her look. Something about her was terrifying, but also beautiful.

Her eyes met just about everyone, but her gaze never left Brutus. She was so attentive, it seemed obsessive, as if she were already in love with him. When their eyes connected, her shoulders relaxed and she gave a small smile before making her way over to him. Brutus's mouth hung open and his eyes glazed over as if he were about to have a heart attack.

"Ay, big man, that lady right there cost a pretty penny," Priapus chimed in, while Brutus still appeared lost in a daze.

"Can't I do him for free?" Pandora asked. "Just this once?"

Priapus's face hardened as he placed his cane on his shoulder.

"What I tell you about loving them for free, huh? You're a nighttime professional working for me, not no street-corner trick, bitch!"

As her face tensed, Pandora seemed to lose some of her coolness for the briefest moment. "But he's so fine though! He shouldn't have to pay for a little bit of fun!"

Priapus stomped his foot and scowled his eyes. "What did I say?"

Perseus laughed nervously. "Priapus, don't even worry about it! I got you on this one!"

Priapus relaxed and he burst out laughing, walking towards Perseus for a handshake. "That's what I'm talkin' about! You've always been good to do business with!"

"All right now everybody, we came in here to get down didn't we?!" Perseus exclaimed, taking some bottles from the bar. He picked up a blunt and lit it as "The Humpty Dance" played in the background. A thick haze began to cover the room as the blunt was passed around and the guys spit their respective games with the ladies, each of whom stared back seductively.

Priapus stood in a corner with a blunt of his own and a glass of cognac in hand. I sat quietly and took everything in, waiting for the moment it was all over, so we could go home. I felt someone staring at me and looked around to see Priapus looking in my direction.

"What's up with you, little bit?" he shouted with a sly smile.

"Hey," I replied coldly, looking away from him.

"Is that how it is?" he laughed, approaching the couch I was sitting on and taking a seat next to me. "Ain't no need to be a flower on the wall!"

"My brother wanted to come here and dragged me along for the ride. This ain't my type of thing."

"I see," Priapus said, nodding his head. "Big yellow man over there?"

"Yup, that's him."

He laughed again. "So, what's the deal with you, anyway?"

I glared at him. "Excuse me?"

He chuckled as he leaned in. "I'm sensing somethin' real powerful from you. Don't get me wrong... it's a good energy, just powerful. Like you got some tricks up your sleeve or somethin'."

"Are you trying to call me a witch?"

"I mean, it's all good if you are!" Priapus shouted, patting me on the shoulder. "I ain't got nothin' against witches! Little sister happens to be one!"

"I see," I said as I moved his hand off my shoulder.

He laughed again and looked me dead in the eye "You act just like my sister too! Here's a word of advice for you: be true to who you really are. The sooner the better. A little somethin' you probably needed to hear with all you been goin' through lately."

"And how would you know what I've been going through?"

"Let's just say I'm a man who has my ways," he chuckled, pointing at his temple.

"Um, okay," I replied quizzically, going back to observing Brutus and the others talking over drinks and blunts.

"So you not gonna join in on the fun?"

"I'm good."

"Live a little!" he enthused, sliding over and shoving his blunt into my mouth. I coughed frantically and waved the smoke away from my face. Strangely enough, I actually kind of liked it. I motioned for him to pass it to me again, which he did with a smile. I had always watched Brutus, so I took another hit and held it in like a natural. Priapus offered me a sip from his cognac glass and I gladly obliged.

The next morning, I woke up on the floor of Brutus's bedroom, but I had no idea how I got there. I looked at the nearest clock and saw that it was 5:45 A.M. Then, I looked towards the bed and saw Brutus and Pandora holding each other tightly while they slept.

The Day After

It was 5:45 A.M. Demeter laid in bed, sleeping away, as Pan sat underneath the orange glow of the lamp at the nightstand, reading an unsent letter.

"No matter what I say or do, these children always find some way to undermine me," he said, placing the letter back in the drawer and making his way to the bathroom.

As the shower's hot water poured onto his skin, he formed a rich lather of soap and thought of the night prior. He let out a guilty sigh as he got out the shower, dried his skin and made his way out of the bathroom. As he opened the bedroom door, he was greeted by the sight of Demeter sitting on the bed, awaiting his return.

"Good to see you still have it," Demeter complimented in a dry tone.

Pan nodded. "I could say the same about you."

"So now you wanna show me love and affection, huh?" Demeter asked sarcastically with a chuckle. "For the last two years or so, it seems the only thing you wanna talk about is how much weight I gained."

Demeter stood up from the bed and put on her robe, stretching quickly before making her way to the bathroom, as Pan eyed her the entire time.

"What's his name?" he blurted out, his voice emitting a slight crack as he finally broke his silence.

Demeter turned to him with a raised eyebrow. "Excuse me?"

Pan nodded, with a tear rolling down his cheek. "You know exactly what I'm talking about! I see a glow on you I haven't seen since we first got married! And I know it ain't because of me!"

Demeter let out a slight laugh. "Like you ain't been sleeping around with these white Royal heifers for years! You'd tried so hard to hide it, but I knew all along. Yet the minute you even *suspect* I'm having an affair, you have to nerve to yell at me, crying like a crocodile!"

More tears rolled down his face as he sobbed. "I can't believe you."

Demeter made her way to the bathroom and began her shower. "Well believe it, baby! And until further notice, you need to sleep in the guestroom." Speechless, Pan sat back on the bed as Demeter started humming in the shower.

* * *

"What happened last night?" I asked, pacing back and forth in Brutus's room as he and Pandora started to wake up.

"Something beautiful," Pandora said sultrily, caressing Brutus's body.

"You can say that again," Brutus laughed, slowly prying his eyes open.

"Guys, I'm serious! The last thing I remember is taking a few hits off of a blunt and sipping some Hennessy! After that, it's all a blank! Do you guys remember what happened?"

Pandora laughed. "You just spaced out on the couch. MC Crius and his crew came through and we had a little party. That's all that happened. Don't worry about it."

Brutus sat up and started kissing Pandora on the neck and she chuckled. "And the two of us made sweet, sweet love."

"Oh yeah, that too," Pandora laughed.

I just stared at them. "You two were doing it while I was in here laying on the floor?!"

Brutus's eyes furrowed. "What kind of bro do you take me for? We went into Julius's old bedroom. We just came back in here to sleep."

"Thank god," I said with a sigh of relief. "How come you two remember so much and I don't remember anything?"

"I don't know, something about the enchantment at that Megalopolis place," Pandora explained, wearing light blue lace lingerie and starting to put her clothes back on. "Some people remember stuff, others don't."

"I don't think I understand," I stammered nervously.

"Who does?" Pandora shrugged, putting on her heels on as Brutus got out of bed, wearing nothing at all.

I shielded my eyes. "Whoa, Brutus! Put some clothes on!"

"Well, you're no fun," Pandora enthused seductively, standing behind him and rubbing his belly. "This man is thick in all the right places. His physique should never be covered with clothes."

Brutus laughed as he put on a pair of jeans. "Ain't no girl ever talked about me like that before."

"I don't see why not! Workin' for Priapus, I've been around the block, baby. There's been guys here and there that were exceptional, but most of the time, it was just work. But there's just something about you that's like no other."

"Oh yeah?" Brutus replied flirtatiously. "Keep talkin' that

talk to me and I may take these jeans off again."

"Um, hello!? I'm right here!" I shouted, cringing at the scene unfolding in front of my very own eyes.

"Ain't nobody told you to stay in here!" Brutus exclaimed, pushing Pandora on the bed. I ran out of the room as they began kissing, being sure to shut the door behind me.

I walked back to my room and decided to check the box again. I opened it to another purple note. The Oracle had gotten back to me.

Dear Calliope,

I'm glad you've obliged! I think it's time for a proper introduction, yes? I am Pythia de Delphi, a daughter of the House of Delphi, but for discretion purposes, I would rather you refer to me as The Oracle. Here's a little history lesson for you: The House of Delphi and The House of Thessaly were two of the seven Sacred Graeae Houses of Trakiya. You come from a bloodline of Mage royalty.

All that aside, you are very important. Your real mother had the potential to evolve from a Mage into a full-fledged Sorceress! I could feel it! Alas, her life was cut tragically short and we never saw that come into fruition. However, due to her love for you and this enchanted box, that potential has been passed down onto you.

I completely understand and respect your request for us to go at the pace you wish. After all, I know this is all new to you. Alas, things are starting to rupture again, so we can't be too easy on time. Just so you know, this piece of parchment you hold is enchanted. As such, I will be made aware when you are holding it and can provide an immediate response to whatever message you have in reply, as if we were holding a conversation over the phone.

I held the paper away from me for a moment. "What does all of this even mean?" I put the piece of paper down and turned it over, contemplating what to write. After a few minutes, I decided to reply with the question I found the most important of all: *So are you saying I'm a witch?*

I quickly refolded it and was about to place it back into the box, when I felt a strange tingling sensation in my fingers. The paper began to emit a glow whilst vibrating. I unfolded the paper only to behold the revelation:

The proper term is Mage, Calliope. We consider the term "witch" to be an offensive slur. But to answer your question: yes, you are a witch. But not just any witch - you're the daughter of the Crimson Maiden.

* * *

"Oh yes, oh yes!" Hadrian yelled as Narcissus tied ropes all over his body in her bedroom. "Oh, oh, oh... *OH YES!*"

In a leather eye-mask and a shiny black robe, Narcissus smiled at him. "Stop screaming like a bitch and yell like a man!"

"As you are my master and I am your slave, whatever you wish!" Hadrian exclaimed between panting breaths, starting to shout with a deeper, more aggressive growl. After a few more minutes of bondage, Narcissus untied the ropes and they laid down on the bed, sharing a post-coital cigarette.

"I forgot how much fun it was to have you dominate me," Hadrian said, taking a hit of the cigarette before passing it.

Narcissus smiled. "Well, I didn't. There's something so potent about the pleasure that comes from pain."

They both laughed. "So, now that you've returned to Griffin, what are your plans?"

Narcissus passed the cigarette back to Hadrian. "It will be as if I've retired. No more politics for me! I'm going to run a flower shop on Ponos Street."

"Is that it? I would think you'd be interested in something a little more... *fun*."

"Oh, of course not!" she laughed with an evil grin and a malicious glare. "There's one area where my work isn't finished: exterminating witches!"

"Ha! That's the Narcissus I know. Do you have any potential leads yet?"

"Well, you remember the Crimson Maiden?'

"Yes. What of it?"

"Did you ever wonder what happened to her baby?"

"I thought you had it thrown in the hot springs of the South Forest?"

Narcissus grew wide-eyed. "Oh heavens no! The thought crossed my mind, but even I couldn't bear to kill a baby! Instead, I requested that Pan Thessaly take her in."

Hadrian raised his eyebrow as Narcissus sat up on the bed and turned away from him. "There were several conditions to the agreement. The first was that her mystic blood be sterilized. The second was that she be kept hidden and shut out from the world until she's of age. Third, he was not to ever speak of her true parentage and keep all talk of Mages and other Mystics to a minimum."

"Anything else?"

Narcissus put back on her grin and stare, as she turned to Hadrian. "The final condition was to hold on to the Crimson Maiden's enchanted box. Hide it from the child, of course, but to never throw it away. That way, the enchantment placed on it would allow me to keep track of where she is at all times. "

Hadrian grimaced as he sat up. "Well, if her sterilization worked, then maybe we'll have nothing to worry about."

"That's the problem! The sterilization only delayed the

process. When I laid eyes upon her the day I moved in, I could feel the magic energy coursing through her veins. We have to do something soon! The last thing Atalan needs is another Crimson Maiden!"

* * *

I began the walk to school, without Brutus, pondering what I had just been told by The Oracle.

"Of all people, how could I be a Mage? I've never even..." I thought back to when I lit the candle on the counter with my own eyes after the night Brutus left the door open again after stinking it up. Just by looking at it. There was no other explanation.

"That passage," I said aloud. The one in Latin. It had to have been a spell. That's why I quickly gained the power to light something on fire. I had actually used magic before.

"Hey Calliope!"

I stopped and turned to see Pandora walking up behind me, with a smile on her face and a cigarette in her hand. Her make-up was still on point, but her hair was a bit untidy.

"Hi," I said quizzically. "Are you happy to see me or something?"

Pandora laughed. "Yes. We're friends now, aren't we?"

"I don't even know you though."

"Oh, well excuse me!" she quipped. "I just thought you'd be a cool person to be around!"

"I guess," I shrugged. "I'm not the best at making friends or talking to people."

"Well, let me change that!" she enthused, reaching into her purse. "You want a cigarette?"

"Sure."

I took the cigarette and turned away from her, holding my hands close to my face to mimic holding a lighter. I squinted and held my hands closer as I incanted the spell in my mind. Suddenly, I could feel a slight heat underneath my hands. I opened my eyes and saw that I had managed to light the cigarette using nothing more than my mind.

"Calliope?" Pandora asked. "It takes you awhile to light a cigarette, huh?"

"It's a little windy today!" I lied while Pandora looked around, waving her hands to feel it. I could tell she didn't believe me, but shrugged it off.

"I guess Brutus ain't comin' to school today, huh?"

"Nope! He had too much fun with me," Pandora boasted.

"Yeah, I noticed." She let out another chuckle as I continued to look at her. "So where are you going?"

"I'm just walking towards the school with you. Priapus said he'd pick me up there."

"I see. So why do you and those other girls work for him anyway? I get the feeling he isn't very nice."

Pandora let out a cough. "He's very nice! He just doesn't like it when something gets between him and his money."

"So it's all about money with him?"

"Not even! That man saved my life! When I was your age, I got disowned and had nowhere to go. Had he not found me on that cold winter night three years ago, I'd still be on the streets."

"He made you a sex slave though."

She side-eyed me. "It ain't even like that, Calliope."

"I'm sorry if I offended you."

"Don't even worry about it," Pandora said with a laugh. "I know you Auburn folks tend to be on the bougie side."

I shrugged it off as the two of us kept walking towards Pegasus

High, before we stopped and sat on a bench in the gazebo park across the street. We finished our cigarettes and talked until Fortuna and Pietas approached us.

"Hey Calliope!"

"Nice to see you, Fortuna," I said with a smile as Pietas and I exchanged head nods.

"Hi strangers," Pandora said with a laugh.

"Hey there," Fortuna said. "Never seen you around this way before."

Pandora laughed again. "I'm not usually out this way. Pandora's the name, straight outta the Cascade."

"Oh yeah?" Pietas added. "Most people around these parts are terrified of you guys."

"Yeah, I know, but I just came out here on business. Matter of fact, that's my ride right there. I'll catch you guys later!"

Pandora left the bench as a late-70s maroon Cadillac Seville with gold-plated rims approached. Priapus rolled down the window in sunglasses and shot a head nod in her direction as she got into the backseat. He drove off, shooting a raised eyebrow and smile in my direction.

"Calliope? Do you know who that is?"

"Yeah, that's Priapus. I met him last night when Brutus took me to The Megalopolis."

Fortuna blinked and shook her hands. "Okay, first off, don't ever go to The Megalopolis again... that place is bad news. Second, stay away from him. And Pandora."

I looked at her sideways. "Why would you say that?"

"I'm being serious! I know all about him! When my cousin Lucina got disowned a couple of months ago, he found her and sweet-talked her into being a prostitute for him! He's not a good person!"

I gasped and stared at her wide-eyed. "Okay, Fortuna. I'll take your word for it." I already felt nervous around him to begin with, but Fortuna's words confirmed my suspicions.

"So you already noticed what was going on with his women then?" Fortuna asked.

I stared at her in shock. "Wait, how did you know what I was thinking that?"

Pietas grew wide-eyed and stepped back. "Again with the mind-reading, Fortuna?"

"I... I don't know." Fortuna said jumpily. "Excuse me guys, I think I need some time alone." She walked across the street as Pietas and I just watched.

"What was that all about?" Pietas asked, sitting down next to me.

"Don't ask me," I said, as we watched her walk into Pegasus High. I looked at my hands for a moment before letting out a sigh and putting them back down.

Still Searching For The Red Light

I sang in my head as I listened to the dial tone. *"One day I'll fly away, leave all this to yesterday"* I had grown tired of waiting for Herc to call me, so I decided to give Leto's Cleaners a call to see what was going on.

"Hello?"

"Hey Leto, it's Calliope," I greeted. "How are you?"

"Hey there, how have you been?" Leto greeted back somberly.

"I've been fine, thanks for asking. Is Herc available?" I asked. "I was wondering why he hadn't called me lately."

Leto was silent for a moment before he sighed. "I hate to break this to you, but I'm afraid I haven't heard from him in weeks."

"What happened?!"

Leto sighed again. "Apollo came home one day with a really bad bruise. He never told me how he got it, but he did tell Herc. He got so mad, he stormed out. A few hours later, he came running back into the house and packed up as much of his stuff as he could. He gave me and Apollo a kiss and a hug and then he left. Haven't seen him since."

"I'm so sorry, Leto."

I hear him sniffle. "Thank you. The next day, some members of the Peloponnesian's security staff barged in and conducted a search. I asked what the meaning of it all was, but they wouldn't tell me. Herc's been tired of putting up with that family's nonsense for a while. Boy would've quit a long time ago if it wasn't for all the bills around here. I don't doubt it one bit that he crossed a line. It was only a matter of time."

"I'm really sorry to hear about all of this, Leto. Wish there was something I could do."

"Thank you, Calliope. I really appreciate that. Just worried about my boy."

"Wherever he is, I hope he's okay."

"Me too, Calliope. Me too. I have to go now, but I'll talk to you later."

Leto hung up and I put the phone back on the receiver with a sigh.

"First Julius. And now Herc? Why is everyone close to me just... vanishing?"

* * *

Brutus neared Pegasus High before deciding to pause and sit at the gazebo park across the street from the school. He sat down at the bench and took a quick look around. He breathed a sigh of relief before reaching into his pocket to pull out a small joint.

"Got any for me?" he heard a girl ask. He turned around to see Pandora approaching with a big smile on her face.

Brutus bobbed his head and smiled before handing it over. "Help yourself."

Pandora smiled and took a hit, breathing it out with a slight cough. "Thank you, baby."

"Oh yeah, anytime," Brutus said flirtatiously, "What brings you out this way? Got another client or somethin'?"

"I wanted to see you again."

Brutus choked and patted his chest. "For real?" Pandora nodded as he put his hands up and laughed. "Well look, I can't say I don't appreciate it, but I don't got any money. I mean, my dad does, but he ain't about to pay for no hooker."

"Who said I wanted you to pay me?"

"Ain't that the whole idea?"

Pandora chuckled. "Remember what I said to you a week ago? About you being like no other? I meant every word of that, baby."

Brutus shook his head. "Oh yeah? I don't think that pimp of yours would approve!"

"What Priapus don't know won't hurt him!" Pandora insisted, pulling Brutus in for a kiss. Brutus closed his eyes and held her tightly and caressed her backside as they continued to kiss passionately. When he opened his eyes and broke the kiss, he spotted Medea staring at him across the street. She glared at him silently as she stood at the edge of the courtyard. She closed her eyes and clenched her teeth before turning around andb storming into the school.

Pandora took note. "Who was that?"

"Just some girl that I used to know," Brutus sighed, looking back at her.

Pandora looked towards her once more, her eyes furrowed into a squint. "She'll get over it. I can tell she don't really care about you anyway. As for me, I care about you a lot. Always have."

"You've *always* cared about me? We just met last week!"

Pandora let out a slight hiccup. "Look, you ain't nobody thinkin' about that rich white bitch, right? Why don't you ditch school for the day and come with me instead?"

Pandora kissed Brutus again, before he smiled. "Alright, shorty! I'm down with that."

He let her have one more hit of the joint before he finished up and stomped it out on the ground, holding Pandora's hand tightly as they left the gazebo.

* * *

Pan pulled up in front of Marcellus's, an Italian restaurant a few blocks away from Ponos Street. It was a structure with a low hanging roof painted a tan-orange shade. Several diners were conversing, enjoying their lunches on the shaded patio as he walked in. The space was dimly-lit, with curtains covering the candlelit booths surrounding the main dining floor. Everything was swathed in shades of indigo and black, including the host's podium, where a chubby, balding man with tan skin and a beard stood.

"*Buon pomeriggio!*" the host greeted enthusiastically in a profound Italian accent. "Table for how many?"

Pan took his hat off and laughed. "I'm actually here to join another party. Could you show me where Narcissus, Romulus and Remus are sitting?"

The host's eyes grew wide before he groaned. "Right this way, sir."

Pan followed as he led him to their table. They were talking at one of the curtain-covered booths with the occasional laugh breaking out between Narcissus's sips of wine. Remus was a skinnier version of Cicero, with a profound hooked nose.

"Right here, sir."

"Thank you very much," Pan said, taking a seat next to Romulus.

The host began to walk away when Romulus him called out. "Hey Fabius!"

Fabius groaned once more, turning to Romulus. "Yes sir?"

"Marcellus always tells us how great of a host you are, and yet whenever the House of Caligula shows up, we never feel any of the love! What's up with that!?"

Fabius stroked his beard. "I love all my guests! Provided they're not patronizing, of course."

Remus smacked his lips. "Patronizing, huh? Okay, listen up, jabonee! The House of Velia has been one of the closest confidants of the House of Caligula for many years! Romulus and I are like family to Marcellus! I'll have you know we don't appreciate that presumption one bit!"

"Very well, sir. My apologies," Fabius said before he walked away, mumbling in Italian.

Remus lit up a cigar and shook his head. "Fucking Sicilians."

Pan sat there silently while Narcissus and Romulus burst out laughing. "Yeah, I never could understand that bunch!" Romulus added.

"Okay, that's enough tomfoolery for now," Narcissus said. "We need to talk over some very important matters with our guest here."

"Right, right, of course," Remus agreed, "I received word from Zeu-se that you are seeking to become a member of the council, is that right?"

Pan smiled. "You heard right. With my experience in architecture and urban design, I think I'd be the perfect fit."

Narcissus took another sip of her wine and smirked. "Not to mention, your hatred of South Atalan and the Mystic classes."

Romulus patted Pan on the back. "Exactly! You're just the man we need! Ever since that truce bullshit, the Mafia here can barely lay a finger on The Cascade these days. But with you as our eyes and ears, that's gonna change soon enough!"

Pan let out a laugh. "I'm very happy to hear that. Glad to know my efforts for the cause are appreciated."

"Oh, definitely!" Remus added. "Raise the rent! Demolish the projects! Do an eviction sweep! Push those damn south-siders out!"

Romulus laughed as he took a hit of his cigar. "Send 'em all running to Baltimore or Hampton Roads where they belong!"

"Oh, they can have them as far as I'm concerned! Here in Atalan, we will have a real utopia," Narcissus said, taking another hit of her cigarette. "A real balance of disorder has been sweeping the nation lately. It appears that no one is willing to stay in their place anymore."

"Just look at what's going on in Los Angeles! Good for nothing titsoons running around, trying to destroy the city just because a cop was doing his job," Romulus said, turning to Pan. "Not trying to lump you in with that pack of animals though."

"I take no offense to that in the slightest," Pan assured. "I've seen the riots on TV myself. Damn shame, running around and actin' foolish just like the south-siders. That's the number one problem with my people across this country. If more of us were noble, upstanding citizens like the people of Auburn and less like those wild, savage animals like the blacks in Inman and The Cascade, we wouldn't have these problems!"

"Nice to know that there's still some members of your group with some sense," Narcissus said with a devious grin. "Let us hope that the concept of freedom our society has had going into the 1990s won't last for long."

* * *

We sat silently in Hestia's class, anxiously awaiting for her to hand out the grades for our poetry assignment. She walked around the class, handing them out one by one, either giving the student a compliment or some sort of suggestion. I gulped as she approached me, eyeing my paper.

"You know, Calliope, this poem was a bit... how should I say this? Rugged and 'around the way' for me."

Eris eyed me mischievously as I nodded. "What exactly do you mean by that, Mrs. Loukas?"

Hestia sighed. "Basically, I found it kind of ghetto."

"Oh," I replied, rolling my eyes into the back of my head.

"However, in all my years of teaching, it has to be one of the best poems I have ever read. I was enamored by how you vividly described the nighttime masquerader and the works of art he weaved with his spray can. Although it describes things I don't think I will ever understand, I can't dismiss fine art when I see it. You get an A+ for this assignment, Calliope. Keep up the good work!"

Much to the shock of everyone in the class, she handed my paper to me and I heard Eris scoff as I smiled, looking down at my paper.

Hestia walked over to her seat next, handing over her paper. "I have a B!? Are you sure this is the right paper, Mom?!"

Hestia bent down to her and smiled. "Eris, how many times do I have to remind you it's Mrs. Loukas at school?"

Some students in the class laughed. "Well, *Mrs. Loukas*, there surely has to be some sort of mistake here! I was studying Remi and Mayo Angelo all week, just so I could write the perfect poem!"

Hestia just laughed. "No piece of writing is perfect, Eris. It's all in the eye of the beholder. You see that Calliope did really well on this assignment... why not go to her for some advice on the next one?"

"Ugh!" Eris groaned as the bell rung. "Fine!" I couldn't help but chuckle as I packed my bag and made my way out of the class. I had almost reached my next class when I felt someone tug on my hair. I gulped when I saw I was face to face with Atropos, who stared at me in maniacal glee, while Eris and Moirai snickered behind her.

"Who gave you permission to touch my hair!?"

The three of them began to laugh boisterously as a crowd began to form. I began to fume at the blatant display of disrespect as a lump in my throat began to form, as it registered that everyone was laughing at me.

"Look, I'm just trying to go to my next class! Why don't you guys just mind your own business!?"

"We could say the same about you," Moirai said. "Eris told us all about you embarrassing her in class."

"A class that just so happens to be taught by my *MOTHER*!" Eris added with a scowl.

"I beg your pardon? I can't help it if I did better on a writing assignment than you did!"

Atropos burst out laughing once more. "So you're an arrogant, Black-American princess with an attitude problem? Color me surprised!"

"Well, she is from Auburn, you know," Moirai said facetiously, looking down at her fingernails as Eris nodded in agreement.

I just rolled my eyes. "Look, I couldn't care less what you, or anyone else in this school thinks. Go ahead and talk about me all you like. If you'll excuse me, I'm about to be late for my next class."

I turned around and made my way back to my class when I heard Atropos yell out. "Not so fast, golliwog!"

She pushed me against the dark yellow, metal lockers in the hallway, dropping my bag and books in the process. I stooped down, scrambling to pick everything up when she stomped down on one of my textbooks.

I looked up to her with a glare. "You chose the wrong clique to mess with! You should have remained invisible, but you wanted to run your mouth, didn't you? Best behave yourself, *Calloser*. We're watching you!"

She looked back to Eris and Moirai. "Looks like it's time for a little meeting in the ladies room. There's probably worms crawling around in her hair... the last thing my nails need is a fungal infection. Come on, ladies!"

I rolled my eyes and shook my head as they walked off. I was still gathering my things when the bell rung suddenly. I ran over to my next class, only to be halted by Principal Erebus.

"Where are we supposed to be right now, young lady?" He asked sternly.

"Sir, I'm sorry, some girls pushed me over when I was walking to class earlier," I explained, before I composed myself and went on to accuse, "One of whom was Atropos."

"Excuse me? Is this your idea of a joke?"

"No, sir! I'm telling you the truth!"

"Young lady, I'll have you know that Atropos is an honors student and an upstanding, model citizen. I do not appreciate your childish attempt at incriminating her!"

"She just bullied me! Principal Erebus, with all due respect..."

"Irrelevant! I was going to tell you to move faster next time, but thanks to your flagrant disrespect, I'm afraid you've just earned yourself a week's worth of detention. Maybe next time you won't be such a troublemaker."

* * *

Fortuna turned on the stereo in her room as she took off her backpack and pounced on the bed. She smoked a cigarette while bobbing her head to Pearl Jam. She put out her cigarette and was about to fall asleep when she heard a knock at the door.

"Go away, please!" she demanded.

"I'm getting real sick and tired of your damn attitude," Cicero scoffed, opening the door and walked in anyway. "I want to talk to you."

Fortuna rolled her eyes. "What now?"

Cicero glared at her as he folded his arms. "Tyche told me about you stealing her car a couple of weeks back. That was some reckless bullshit, even by your standards! I want you to explain yourself!"

Fortuna's eyes widened as she promptly sat up in bed. "You're just now hearing about that? I know I joked around you two only talking once a month, but I had no idea it was literal."

"That's none of your damn business!" Cicero shouted, pointing his finger at her. "I came to your room because I wanted to know what the hell came over you, huh? What the fuck compelled you to steal a car for a joy ride in the middle of the night?!"

"I don't know... I was just bored!" Fortuna explained hurriedly, trying to shoo Cicero away. "Just go away already."

Cicero rolled his eyes and sighed before taking a seat on her bed. "Listen, you act like I don't care about you, but believe me, I do. I didn't come in here to yell at you. But you could have gotten in a crash. Or gotten pulled over and arrested because you don't have a license! Did you even think about that?"

Fortuna sighed and twiddled her fingers. "I understand. I'm

sorry."

"Thank you. Please don't do anything like that ever again. What were you doing with her car anyway? Hanging out with that new friend of yours?"

"Yes, I was with Calliope."

Cicero chuckled. "Seems like you've really been enjoying your time with her."

"Wait, you actually approve?" Fortuna asked with her eyebrows raised in confusion. "I thought you didn't like her?"

Cicero shook his head and sighed. "Look, I know you've been really lonely since Lucina got disowned. I'm just happy you finally found someone to call a friend."

"Thanks, I really appreciate that," Fortuna said, slowly starting to smile.

"Of course," Cicero replied, with a laugh. "You always were the antisocial type. What's so different about her?"

Fortuna twiddled her fingers. "I always feel like everyone goes straight to judging me. She was the first girl I met who didn't do that. It felt so good to talk to her because her thoughts didn't have anything negative to say about me."

Cicero turned to her. "Didn't I tell you I don't want you to say anything about reading other people's minds?"

"You know I can't help it sometimes!"

"Just block it out or something!" Cicero insisted angrily.

"You know what, just leave!" Fortuna shouted as she pointed at the door, "Every time you start acting like a dad again, I say one thing that upsets you and you go right back to being a hostile mobster! It never fails!"

"Shit!" Cicero whispered to himself before apologizing, "Look, Fortuna, I'm sorry. I didn't mean to lash out at you like that. I never do."

"Yeah right!" Fortuna retorted. "You always apologize only to do it again the next day! It's like there's something in you that's missing!"

"There isn't anything missing in me!" Cicero pleaded as he got off her bed. "If anything, there's something inside that I wish would go away!"

"Ugh!" Fortuna groaned, before she closed her eyes. *"Cuando se pone difícil, solo recuerda de dónde viniste."*

Cicero's eyes practically bulged out of his head. "How do you know that phrase?"

Fortuna shrugged. "It's something I remember a man saying to me when I was really little."

Cicero took a step back and looked down to reminisce. "She used to say the same thing, all the time."

Fortuna sat up in her bed to look at him intently. "You mean Pleione?"

Cicero just shook his head and dismissed the thought. "You know I don't like to talk about that woman."

"Why the hell not?!" Fortuna pleaded. "You always liked her better than mom. Hell, she was more of a mother to me than mom ever was."

"That's exactly why!" Cicero snapped as he pointed at her. "Matter of fact, just forget this whole conversation!"

Cicero rubbed the back of his head and sighed as he walked out of Fortuna's room, closing the door behind him. Fortuna spaced out for a moment before opening the drawer to her nightstand and taking out a photo album. While a single tear fell down her face, she couldn't help but smile as she looked upon the photos of herself and Cicero in happier times. She chuckled at the pictures of him when he had more hair and a skinnier build, as well as the old-fashioned, frilly dresses that she and Lucina wore at the family reunion.

On the last page, she paused to look at a photo of her with a woman and another kid dated back to 1981. She was a tall woman with dark, tawny skin, big lips, a broad nose and long, wavy black hair, with the young boy looking very similar to her with a slightly lighter skin tone and very curly hair. They were all smiling bright and wide in front of a half-eaten pizza at an arcade.

"You two cared about me more than the House of Caligula ever did." A tear slowly trickled down her face as she sighed and laid back down in bed.

* * *

I twiddled my fingers, laying in bed with the box next to me. I was awaiting a message from The Oracle. I sighed while looking up at the ceiling of my room as a lump in my throat grew. I thought back to the very first note I had read. The one where the other Calliope spoke of setting someone on fire. That was exactly what I wanted to do to Atropos, Eris and Moirai.

Suddenly, the purple parchment began to glow and vibrate. My heart pounded as I unfolded it quickly and began reading.

Ah, Calliope, don't you think I'm a little bit too old to be a mediator for teenage drama? These girls sound quite insufferable, so I can't say I object to your desire to set them on fire, but alas, you've read the anecdotes of the box, yes? Given the nature of Atalan society, it would be unwise to do any sort of witchcraft in public. I already feel the beginnings of another Rupture coming along and it's best not to rush it. Especially given your location.

By the way, I'm glad you've been practicing. Alas, lighting up cigarettes, matches, candles and stovetops with your mind can only get you so far. Hand conjuring is the prize. I assume you remember the spell you read? The bread and butter of any good Mage, is to become so good with a recipe that you wouldn't even need to recite it in full while conjuring.

Fire is only one of many elements, albeit one of the most powerful. Master the element of flame and the others will come to you in no time. I'd suggest working on that immediately.

It is time for me to retire for the evening. We can speak again in the morning. I bid you adieu, Calliope.

I smiled a little as I placed the note back in the box. I began to wave my hand around, but nothing happened. I started tapping my foot and noticed a glow, as a light emitted from my foot. I stepped back and saw that the light had been magically implanted into the floor.

"Step on the light again," I heard a voice whisper in my ear. I felt chills reverberate throughout my body and they quickly warmed up when it registered that it was the voice of the woman from my visions.

I did as she said and stepped on it once again, as two more lights appeared in front of it, leading to the door. I let out a curious laugh as I followed them and opened my door.

"That's right, baby," she said. "Follow the lights." I stepped on the light in front of the door and a series of lights appeared down the hallway. I followed them to the door at the end of the hallway, leading to the rooftop balcony. I stepped on the light in front of that door and the lights then led up staircase. I looked back and gulped when I saw that all the lights were gone just as suddenly as they had appeared.

"Relax, it's just the magic at work," the voice assured. "Keep following the lights."

"Yes, mother," I said, following the lights up the staircase.

I closed the door behind me and walked up to the rooftop as I looked up at the starlit sky.

"You remember the fire recipe from the box, yes?" the voice inquired. "Just repeat those phrases in your mind and all it takes is a flick of the wrist,"

I nodded. "Ignis, possedi ardens," I began incanting, repeating the passage in my thoughts. I repeated the passage innumerable times and began to feel heat radiating from my hand. I immediately opened my eyes and witnessed a perfectly spherical ball made of flames in my hand, encased in red swirling ribbons. At first, I was shocked, but I relaxed and allowed myself to become one with the warmth, witnessing the miracle that had formed in my hands.

"Very good, daughter," the voice enthused. "While everyone is still asleep, throw it up to the sky!"

I chuckled and my eyes beamed with excitement. Without very much force, I threw the ball of fire high enough for it to reach the stratosphere, when it suddenly burst into a sparkling, golden firework, illuminating the entire night sky. I looked towards the Atalan skyline, and for the briefest moment, I saw the red light, revolving the same as it always did.

The light show lasted no more than a minute. Once it was over, all the details of the Atlantic Colony, including the red light, were obscured into darkness once again with my eyes and heart full of light.

"Fantastic job, Calliope!" the voice said with elation. "You've officially begun your journey as a Mage!"

"Bring the journey on!" I exclaimed, looking up to the sky once more.

About the Author

P. Curry has been writing fiction and poetry ever since he was in elementary school, with some of his work finding its way into college publications. A proud child of the 1990's, and lover of music, history and culture, he spends his free time blogging about these things in his hometown of Las Vegas, Nevada.

You can connect with me on:
- https://twitter.com/p_storyteller
- https://www.facebook.com/pcurrywrites/